MW01127331

The Rest Is Still Unwritten

A Novel by Mark Vertreese

ISBN-10:1508863393
ISBN-13: 978-1508863397

DEDICATION

To everyone who has a story to tell, whether they know it or not.
To Michelle who helped me keep this concept of a 'Companion Autobiography' a secret and pushed me to make sure Janine became a reality.
To anyone who thinks they have nothing to teach the world; live out loud…you might just be someone's inspiration!

June 4

I don't know how I'm supposed to start this. Hell I don't know what in the hell I'm even supposed to say. And I sure as hell don't know why I ever agreed to even do this. I ain't a writer. I don't do shit like this. Never have. And it just sounds dumb to me. And it sounds like a bad idea. And it sounds like a complete damn waste of my time and whatever else. But…whatever. I said I'd do it, so that's what I'm gonna do. I guess.

Um, okay so what do you want to know about me? And what the hell do I want to tell you? To start, it's June 4th. My name is Janine. I'm a chunky but sexy 60 year old black woman. I'm on death row. Been here for over twenty-seven years, eight months, and fifteen days now. Yeah, I still count. Don't know why. Oh, and the kicker? I'm gonna be dead in 30 days.

Ain't that some shit?

I really don't know where to start. Sister said I should just write what's in my head. And that was in my head. Sister said a lot of stuff before she left earlier today. I don't know how much of it I was supposed to remember. I honestly don't even give a shit. But it seemed kinda important to her that I do this. Or at least that I try. Why it matters so damn much to her is beyond me. Why does she care more about this than I do?

She kept sayin that this is your legacy. She said it like four or five times before she must have figured out I didn't know what in the fried fuck she was gettin at. Legacy ain't exactly part of my normal choice of words. Sister's old like me, but she still a fancy, kinda messed up white girl do-gooder, so I figure legacy roll out of her mouth like water off a duck.

She told me that whatever I write in this thing about my life is gonna live on past me. When they kill my ass, what I write means somethin.

Like they'll never be able to silence me – my voice is gonna live on forever. My legacy. Hot damn, look at that. I used that bitch in a sentence! Anyway, that was some deep shit and I told her that I understood even though I didn't get it until just now. Sometime you gotta do that with Sister. Let her think you know what she talkin about, go on about your business, and then think on the shit later when she's gone. At least that's how I do it. She might be doin shit completely different.

I still don't understand why the hell I can't just talk and her write the shit down. Like one of them secretaries back in the day when bosses smoked in the office, and bitches had dinner on the table when their man got home. I talk, she writes. Simple. I never knew how secretaries used to be writin so fast. No way they got it all down. I bet half the time they made some shit up, nodded like they knew what the boss was talkin about and moved on. Ha. Just like I do with Sister. Must have been some lyin ass bitches back in the day. So I'm gonna write, give whatever I write to Sister and she gonna do whatever she gonna do with it.

But all I got is me. No secretary, no nobody. Seem like it's been like that my whole life. I can't really remember when I ever had somebody real to lean on. Not for long, anyway. People was always comin and goin, leavin me to fend for myself or take care of myself. Sister's about the only one I can think of whoever cared. Or told me. Or showed me. I used to think she wanted somethin from me. Like I was a project or a bet or somethin. I was supposed to smile when I saw her ass in the visitation room or durin our sessions in her office before I got sent up here to bitch ass Death Row, answerin her stupid questions while she wrote down what I said in a little notebook.

I told her one time early on I didn't want her writin down nothin I said from now on. Didn't seem right to me keepin no notes on me. And she stopped. She actually listened to me and stopped. That freaked my ass out even more. Nobody ever listened to me or gave a damn about what I wanted until her. I didn't know how to take it. I think I liked it, though. I liked the way it felt to have somethin done that I wanted, somethin done just for me and because I said it. I ain't tell Sister that. But I liked it.

In 30 days, some coward asshole behind a curtain is gonna push a button and some freaky, nasty shit is gonna get pumped into me. Sister thought she was bein kind or whatever when she explained to me what was gonna to happen. Like she was puttin my mind at ease if I knew the particulars and the names of the drugs they gonna use. Wrong, bitch. Dead ass wrong. How would you like it if I told you how and when you're gonna die? That's what I asked her. Shut that ass right on up. I felt bad after that when she started to cry. That wasn't what I was trying to make her do. She knew it, I guess. Somethin else was wrong, but she didn't let it out. It wasn't me. That I know.

Sister reached across the table. Well, she really was sittin next to me, so I guess she reached down the table, if that fuckin matters. She reached down the table and patted my hand and rubbed it a bit. I remember how soft she was. It was nice to feel another person who wasn't hittin or pushin or shovin my fat ass around. The guard yelled at her and she snapped her hand back like I was gonna bite the son of a bitch off and put it back in her lap. But she was still cryin.

I can still smell the pretty lotion she uses. Hell, I still smell it cause she still uses it. But that day, it stayed on my hand for a real long time before it got covered up by some prison stank or whatever was shittier and smelled worse than her. I didn't care if nobody saw me, and I smelled my hand a lot until the pretty was gone.

A lot of people say they'd want to know when they're gonna die. That's bullshit. Up one side and down the other. They never been on death row. And, yeah, motherfuckers can stay here for a long ass time – years and decades sometimes. Right now, there's three of us here - me, Carlette and Blanche. They got room for seven, but it's only us right now until somebody else fucks up. Oh, and everybody's the same, right? Ain't nobody did the shit they accused of. And everybody tryin to get off of death row. Draggin out appeals and court until the sun don't shine. Most everybody figures it ain't gonna work, but then again, shit gets crazy sometime and you might get off with a bad DNA sample or shitty police work. I actually did the shit I'm gonna die for. And I'd do it again if I had to. I went along with the appeals, though. Never know what the hell could happen. I don't got no clue about Carlette and Blanche as we don't speak. And that's fine by me.

You poke along, watching TV in the dayroom down the hall, eat your three squares, and sit in front of your lawyer while he hems and haws about appeals and other shit that don't matter, just watchin him talk, shuttin the world out, and make up your own words while his pretty lips move. For twenty-somethin hours every day but Tuesday, I sit here in this tiny beige ass cell lookin at my hard-ass bed, my little silver shitter and sink, and stare at the wall. I started drawin again recently, maybe like fifteen years ago, because Gonzales – he the nicest guard up here – found out I like to do that and he got me some paper and crayons. Can't give a bitch some markers or some charcoal? I'ma kill myself with a blue marker or eat some charcoal? Damn. Nope. Crayons like a little kid waitin on his food at a restaurant, shuttin his ass up so the adults can talk.

Sometime you look at what I draw and you got to look hard to realize that I only had some crayons. Sit on your ass for almost thirty years and you get pretty fuckin creative when it comes to passin your time. Real talk. What else I got? Um, I got a radio I use to listen to my music and the news. I used to watch TV down the hall in the dayroom, but shit got depressin. They cut off certain channels, and after a while it just seemed like all we could see was the news. Same news I get over the radio, but it ain't as horrible just listenin to it as opposed to watchin the shit unfold on television. People be dyin for no reason. That World Trade Center shit disturbed me to the point I was havin nightmares. So I just stopped watchin TV altogether.

I mind my business and keep to myself. Don't ask me why but they thought it'd be a good idea that I had a job. So every Tuesday, I get walked down through Gen Pop, paraded past the regular criminals, and into the library where I sit behind a grate and hand bitches books they don't know how to read or understand. That's the only time I see anybody but Carlette and Blanche. And, no, I don't speak to none of those regular bitches, neither.

And then the day comes when you get that letter from the Secretary of Public Safety, Commissioner of the Adult Correction Division, and the Director of Prisons. That's the worse day of your life. It's the day you find out how much time you got left, be it 15 or 120 days. And that's for people who can read. That letter means ain't nothin more you or your pretty-lipped lawyer can do. Set in stone. Period, point blank. This is it. I grabbed that letter out of my lawyer's hand and read that bastard out loud. Imagine if you was some piece of shit who ain't learn to read. All you can do is sit there while somebody who's gonna get up, walk out of that fuckin visitation room and go back to their perfect little life reads to you like a little ass baby boy colorin his menu waitin on his chicken nuggets!

It's like bein in the courtroom all over again and somebody readin out your fate like it's nothin. Like whatever they say don't count for shit cause you the one payin the price. Does the jury have a verdict? Yes. Well I got a verdict, too, motherfuckers. The verdict is you all a bunch of punks who don't know me and what I been through. Gonna sit there and read off some bullshit about me being guilty and not one of you bitches and assholes know a thing about me. But you gonna send my black ass to prison for some shit you think I done cause the lawyer for the state tricked your ass, and the police be lying on the stand, but what I gotta say ain't shit. Hell no. Fuck them, fuck you, and fuck that. I knew they was about to tell me I was guilty, but I sat tall and proud, starin each of them on that jury into they soul. I hope that scared the shit out of all of them.

I took that letter and read it myself. Loud and proud. Nobody gonna read to me and tell me when I'm gonna die.

But coming back to my story, Sister was right next to me when I read my letter. She's been there for me longer than anybody. Real talk. She was just kinda readin over my shoulder but she didn't say nothin. She just started cryin. My lawyer said he was sorry. He's the fourth lawyer

I've had. They come and go doin free work because they have to or because they tryin to make a name for themselves or because I don't know why. They just doin their job, really. This latest one been with me for a couple years now. He a cute little chocolate thing, I swear he is. I know good and well I'm old enough to be his Gran, but he ain't never treated me like that, he always even with me, never said a mean or soft thing to me. Chocolate – that's what I call him - was always all business from the jump, even though he knew it was a dead end. I told him he was fired, and then we all started laughin. Not like a real laugh. Like when some awkward shit goes down and nobody knows what to say. Like that. He sat there for a minute and stood up to take his chocolate ass back to his wife or whatever. Hell he could be gay for all I know. We never talked about him, his life, and the shit he liked in all this time. We just talked about trying to get my ass off death row. I ain't even want to talk about gettin let out, cause I knew that shit wasn't gonna happen. Just don't kill my ass. That's all I really wanted. But that went up in smoke.

Anyway, Chocolate got up and left. Sister stayed. She had this look on her face like she was tired or somethin. I can't place it. Like she had somethin on her heart. Crazy white bitch. HaHa. I just read the time and date the state was gonna murder my ass and she the one cryin! Ain't that some shit?

That's when she told me to do this. Write, Janine, she said. Write down everything you can remember. Write down the shit that makes you laugh (she ain't say shit, but you get it). Write down the shit that makes you cry. Let the world know you. Then she started cryin again. And she reached out with that soft lotion hand and touched my hand, rough and ashy and black and Gonzales yelled at her. He nice, but he don't play that. Sister got up. Nah, it was more like she jumped up real quick and walked out the visitation room, face drippin with tears and snot and tellin me to write.

So I guess that's what I'm gonna do.

☠♏⊠♦

Dear Diary –

I listened today as a woman read out loud the date and place and time of her death. It was excruciating for me. As selfish as that sounds – and is – it was the most difficult thing I have experienced throughout the many, many years with her and in my role as her counselor. It pained me in a way I couldn't emote. I was reduced to tears, sobbing by myself as I sat next to a soul whose time on earth had been crisply communicated in black and white. She read proudly, confidently, if a bit showy and sarcastically, strong. But she read. And I was crying.

I know I wasn't supposed to, but I reached for her after she'd finished. Her lawyer had fled, no longer able to fend off the wolves who had come for her. I sensed the relief in his eyes as he turned at the door, presumably looking at Janine for the last time. He was free. The irony was gutting.

He won't show at the execution. The young ones never do. They haven't been hardened to this kind of extreme loss yet, and that is something he should hold on to as long as possible. That's the kind of man he is, but I won't assign any judgment to him for that; not wanting to witness the murder of someone you've grown to care for deeply, someone you've spent hours and months and years trying to protect, someone you'd attempted to guide and to whom you'd ministered, if not using the word of God expressly, but the voice within. All of that falling on deaf ears at times, you knowing that the person who's sat with you, and expressed herself and smiled at the mention of her children or laughed at a funny picture of them when they were little, possibly oblivious to the fact that mommy isn't there now. He, and so many like him are free to live their lives, saying good-bye at the door and good-bye forever, while I and others like me sit and try to digest the pain of it all, living out our own sentences, self-imposed though they may be.

I reached for her hand to steady my own heart, to slow its merciless beating and to temper the aching that was spreading across my body. I needed to feel her soul, her heart beating quickly, given away by the pulsing of her wrist. I needed to feel the warmth of her skin and feeling the love of God washing over her in a time of need never greater than right then at that moment. The angry voice of Gonzales yelling at me, an admonition, that the condemned were not to be touched was like thunder from heavens. It was frightening. I understand his motives in protecting his job, and I know he cares very deeply for Janine, but his tenor and directness, which I had not previously witnessed, still deeply scared me. So much was going wrong in so short a space of time. I was reeling.

In thirty days…. I couldn't even bring myself to finish that sentence. Not then and not now.

Write, I implored. I begged her to write. Leave this world on your terms, with your voice defiant and descriptive and passionate. Resonate just as crisply in the same black and white used to condemn you to death. Live in your experiences. Stand as a child of God in a garden of truth and inspiration. Show women, young and old, the path toward salvation and the way out of a life you so preciously wish you had the chance to relive. Write, Janine, and help a young girl avoid the traps Satan set for you, and keep her from the same fate.

Write and help God save a life.

June 5 (29)

Okay, now what? I still don't really know how this works. Just talk about myself? Maybe I'll wait until I see Sister later today She'll know what to tell me.

☠♏☒♦

Dear Diary –

Did you ever have a dream so realistic you could believe it was truly real? I woke up this morning, extremely frightened, because I was dying. Or at least that's what it felt like. Or, perhaps, how I imagined it to feel.

I was strapped to a table in a bright, white room. A faceless man stood next to a panel of switches, his hand hovering delicately over them like a child patiently playing a game of some sort. With a loud whoosh, the curtains of the viewing room which separated it from my death chamber, were pulled quickly open wide and the gallery stared back at me. Bloody or fat, skinny or smiling – each person was somehow disfigured, somehow grotesque, and hard to look at. Laughing and crying and pointing at me viciously, I suddenly recognized them all. They were me, and I them.

In various forms, at various stages of the life I remembered, and for some horrible reasons, collected there in that voyeuristic and hellish gallery – they sat waiting for me, for us, to die.

☠♏☒♦

Sister came today. It ain't all lollipops and rainbows on death row, in case you was wonderin. I don't exactly have freedom to walk my ass around. But whatever. Guards have been nicer since I got my letter. Martinez brought me a new pillow once – that's how I got to know her. I used to think she wanted more, and I told her, I say oh hell no, bitch, I don't get down like that. Martinez just laughed and told my old ass to take the pillow. She said she was married and ain't want some old ass black bitch no way when her husband put it to her better than anybody else. That shit cracked me up. That was about seven years ago and we fast friends. Y'all already heard me talk about Gonzales. I think he some sweet Puerto Rican carmel, but he could just as well be Mexican. Don't know, don't care. He the sweetest to me. Got me this pen and paper so I can write this down for Sister. That's the kind of stuff I been gettin, and more, since my date came down. Me and Martinez and Gonzales all fast friends. Well, as fast as you can be when one of you behind bars and gonna die. Also had Gregg bring me an extra blanket yesterday. But he look like he want somethin in return. Damn. Couldn't be nice to a sister before we all knew the when and where, but fuck it.

Anyway, Sister came today. She ain't have that much to say. That's odd. Not like her. Days she sit and listen to me complain, and days she makes me stop talkin so she can tell me some preachy shit I don't really want to hear. She always has somethin to tell me. HaHa. I told her she looked like she ain't sleepin good. She just smiled and asked me how I was doin. Was I holdin up? One more day gone I told her. I don't know what it was about me sayin that, but I think it pissed her off.

What did you write yesterday, Janine, she asked me. She was all up in my face and waggin her skinny, wrinkled white finger at me. I told her a long time ago you don't do that shit to me. Nobody gonna put a finger in my face. You gonna draw back a nub, lady, I told her the first time years and years ago. I was younger and had been dropped in her office for counselin – oh, this was way before they put my ass on death row. I been knowin Sister a long ass time. I told her again today to put that goddam finger away. But the first time, a long time ago, she looked me in the eye and got up from her desk. Never stopped lookin at me and ain't never once put that finger back where I told her it belonged. Bitch sat her finger on my nose and told me that if I thought I was stronger than God to push her finger away.

She looked down when she heard my handcuffs rattle. My hands was chained together and then to the chair so I couldn't get to her no way. Sister pushed my head backward and put her skinny finger on my forehead talkin about, the choices you make are yours. The power to let you make them comes from God. Don't you threaten me. Don't you tell me I'm gonna draw back a nub. Think. Use your brain. Your hands couldn't help you. All you had to do to get my finger off your nose, she said, was move your head. That shit hit me wrong for the rest of the day. All she had to damn say was make better choices. Damn. I still smile when I think about that.

Anyway, she asked me today what I wrote and I told her nothin. And she got her face all twisted around like she did when she got mad at other people in the visitation room or like she used to when I sat in her office, or maybe Satan. Hell, I don't know. I said, oh I know you ain't mad at me. No, ma'am. You can take that funny little look and shove it up your ass. The guard on duty gonna clear his throat like that was gonna make me back down. Whatever. I just looked at him and rolled my neck. Know what she said to me? I was wastin my life away in silence. She said in 28 days, you gonna wake up and it's gonna be your last day on earth. You will dwell for eternity in the Kingdom of Heaven as a child of God. But right now, today, this moment, these last 28 days, you have a responsibility. And you're wasting it.

I asked her a responsibility to do what? And she said to teach. I didn't know what to say. I thought maybe she was gonna yell at me or quote some shit from the Bible. She just looked at me.

I thought about it and Sister just kept lookin at me in my face. Like she was trying to scare a yes or whatever out of me. Nobody never asked me to teach. Sister and my kids when they was little is the only ones who even seemed to give a damn about me. For all these years, knowin what kind of person I was and probably am right now. She asked me what I taught my girls. And I told her nothin. They was three and five when I got locked up for good. That's almost too young to even know me real good. And I don't blame them. I mean how are they supposed to know me? I'm as much a stranger to them as they was to me. I ain't really have time to teach them a thing. Nothin good anyway.

Don't waste this opportunity then, Janine, she told me. Don't let yourself waste away, don't let your spirit or your passion atrophy. I had to look that one up, to be honest with you. Atrophy? Damn.

I told her I didn't even know how to do what she wanted. And who wanted to read about my life anway? It's my fuckin life and I didn't want more of it, either. I ain't even know where to start. How do I tell my story, whatever it is, and teach at the same time? Sister told me to break it down, tell it in chunks. Start, middle, and the end. Fine.

I don't know about being no child of God, but….but I'll do it I told her. But you gotta tell me what to write. Nope she said – write what you want. This isn't my story. Only you know your life. Only you know what happened to bring you here time after time. Write. Share. Teach. I asked her where in the hell I was supposed to start. You know what that skinny bitch said? At the beginning. Haha! I hate skinny bitches.

☠♏☒♦

Dear Diary –

I don't know what it was about today. Something magical happened, but I'm unable to put my finger on it. One of the guards said it was nice to see me smile. I think it was Benjamin. Had it been that long? Was smiling something foreign to me and my co-workers so much so that mentioning its return was cause celebre? I smiled more broadly at the compliment – though it was really just an observation – before the significance of it all sank in.

Which one of the faces was I now? Which one had I been when the guard noticed me? Which one had I been that morning when speaking to Janine, giving her direction and pushing her to write?

What is it that *I* am doing?

The Start

June 6 (28)

I was born in a crossfire hurricane. Haha. I don't even know what the hell that is. Jagger must have been on that stuff when he wrote that shit. Don't even make any fuckin sense. Crossfire hurricane. Hell, maybe that would have been better, I don't know.

For real, I was born a long ass time ago in North Carolina. My current residence is the North Carolina Correctional Institution for Woman in Raleigh – and has been for several decades. I was born in Charlotte back when it wasn't nothin special, nothin to look at. I got a bitch of a momma – everybody called her Momma Gloria. Never saw or met my real daddy. I got a dead sister and a living sister. I got two kids. I ain't seen them since before I got put on death row.

I'm sixty years old, and I ain't never gonna be sixty-one. My birthday is July 8. I don't like chocolate or licorice. I'm a little extra tall that I must have got from my daddy, and I'm a little extra on weight that I can tell you for sure I got from my momma. I can't remember the last time I got down with my man, and truth be told, I don't know I miss it all that damn much. I wear my hair in a natural and I love classical piano. I know, that's some crazy shit, ain't it? Me and some snooty ass piano music? I never learned, but that's the one thing I always thought about. I was gonna buy me a piano, and learn how to play some classical shit and blow people's minds. I don't know what it is. Makes me feel high class and smart when I listen to it. I turn on my little radio and it makes me forget where the fuck I am when I listen to it. It's probably the one thing I'm gonna miss about livin.

What else about me you need to know? Well, I look like Diana Ross in The Wiz, all brown and gorgeous, but after she ate the scarecrow, and put on a hundred extra pounds! I got big brown eyes and I got a scar I caught from Momma Gloria runnin down the left side of my face from my temple to the lobe of my ear.

Sister said tell you about me through experiences. So maybe I'll start with that one.

☠♏☒♦

I can't say as I remember everything about this when it happened. A lot of times, people tell you stuff or go through stories in their head and look at you like you supposed to know what happened, to play along or whatever. I did that for a long time before I told myself that it just didn't make no damn sense. Why am I pretendin for you? You don't care if I remember what you're talkin about or not, so if it ain't ringin no bells for me, it ain't ringin no bells.

Momma Gloria was bad for that. She liked to tell stories and look you in the face, waitin on you to nod or somehow agree with her that she was tellin it the right way. That used to piss Herbert off somethin good. Oh, Herbert is my step-daddy. You could tell sometime that he didn't give two penny's worth of shit about what Momma Gloria was talkin about. He'd be lookin off into the distance, probably comin up with ways he could kill her or cut out her tongue or some sick shit like that. She'd just be jawbonin like she had to get it out or she'd explode.

Momma Gloria would take a breath and look at Herbert and whack him upside the head. Herbert you damn son of a bitch, you'd better damn listen to me when I'm talkin. I don't know where she was born, but I know it was in North Carolina. And she talked kinda funny. Not like somebody from the south, but like she had piece of candy in her mouth and the words were fightin her tongue to get out. We used to make fun of Momma Gloria and play somethin we called the talkin game. Hold up. The WE I'm talkin about is me and Shaniqua, my little sister. I'ma tell y'all more about her later.

Somebody would be Herbert and they pretend they lookin at somethin, or close they eyes. Whoever played Momma Gloria would be chatterin away like a magpie. Then they'd look over at whoever was supposed to be Herbert and give him down the road. Haha! That was always funny until we got caught. Momma Gloria knew how to fight and she ain't spared us none of the kindness in that regard she should have toward her children.

I say I can't remember everything cause a lot of it's blurry. We'd just got caught by Momma Gloria playin the talkin game. I know it was rainin outside and we played in the house cause she ain't want us trackin mud back inside when we came in for supper. We lived in a little white house, two-story, on the corner with a small little yard and some trees that always dropped more leaves in the fall than me or Shaniqua figured they could hold. I remember we were in the middle of a hill – the bus stop was down at the bottom and the back way to Wayne's grocery store was at the top. We had a bunch of neighbors and kids to play with when we were coming up. It was a neat little place, nothin to talk about, really, that I lived in for a long time.

I think she must of come upstairs to tell us dinner was on when she heard. The house only had two bedrooms. One was for Momma Gloria and Herbert, and the other for me and Shaniqua. We slept in the same room – and when we didn't go outside, that's where we played. We was good and into the game when the door bust open. I thought I saw fire comin off of Momma Gloria. She looked like a demon. Guess cause I was the oldest, she figured I was the ring leader and was the one tellin the golden child we oughta make fun of her. Swear to God I never saw it comin.

When I woke up, Shaniqua had snuck in the room and was rubbin my hand. Kinda like how Sister was doing when I read my letter from the Secretary and whoever else. She was rubbin my hand and I asked her where I was. She laughed and said I was home, sleep. She said Momma Gloria went ape shit on me. She ain't say ape shit cause she was little. I said that for emphasis. That's some other shit Sister told me I should do when I write. Not make it plain, but make it say with emphasis. Don't lie, she said, but make it with emphasis.

Anyway, Momma Gloria busted my head with a book. Threw that son of a bitch across the room and hit me right between my ear and eyeball. That's where I got this scar from. Split my head. And that bitch had the nerve to be mad at me cause I was bleedin on the floor. She the one hit me!

Shaniqua said she thought I liked to die, it scared her to death. Momma Gloria was yellin at her to go down and eat. She never even asked her about me, all slumped over in the floor, bleedin on shit, cause she didn't want to catch a book, either. Herbert came runnin and scooped me up. Took me to somebody he knew about stitchin cuts and stopped the bleedin. Herbert came back and popped Momma Gloria one time in the mouth for that shit. He put me in the bed and then made her heat up his dinner again. I smiled when Shaniqua told me that, but it wasn't the first time he'd put his hands on Momma Gloria, and we all knew it sure enough wasn't gonna to be the last. I seen him hit her before, but never cause of what she done to me. And trust a sista when I say she ain't never gonna be mistaken for no angel. Ever.

I don't know why Herbert slugged her, but I was glad he did. That made me smile for a long time. I see this scar on my face, feel how deep it is cause whoever Herbert took me to didn't know what in the thousand fucks they were doin when they sewed me up, and think about that night. Thanks to Shaniqua I got a picture in my mind of what happened. But I'd rather have heard the punch and watched her big old eyes bug out myself. I'm a grown ass woman, and it still makes me smile to this day. Go ahead, Herbert. Haha. Go ahead.

Some of you people who read this gonna think my Momma Gloria probably wasn't all that bad, that maybe she raised me with a heavy hand cause that's all she knew.

I said that like I really think somebody gonna read this. Sister, you did it again. Tricked my ass into believin somethin just cause you said it. Your ass should have been a magician or a politician or some shit. Damn.

Anyway, Momma Gloria ain't half what I'm telling you. If Satan had a helper on earth, her name was Momma Gloria. And we all sure as hell know that from the bottom of our souls. Somebody on TV used to say from the rooter to the tooter. That always made me laugh, and it's true. From the rooter to the tooter, Momma Gloria was one person nobody liked to see comin. Sister told me to use descriptives when I talk about people, so here's Momma Gloria.

I got to see Color Purple once, or maybe it's The Color Purple, I don't know (and don't care). Remember Oprah was in it, and she was married to some little weak ass brother. What's her name, um, Whoopi told that little man to hit Oprah and he did it. And she tore his ass right on up. Well, the next thing Whoopi know, here comes Oprah, mad as hell and stompin through the corn fields. Bitch looked like a big ass bull knocking everything outta her way to get to Whoopi. She had that I'ma kill your ass look smeared across her face. Her hair was eight kinds of jacked up, and I think the bitch might have been dirty. Well, without the dirty part, that was Momma Gloria. Always mad at somebody, always wantin to fight. She just ain't as clever with the words as Oprah. All my life, I's had to fight. I love that line. Hell, all my life I's had to fight, too. It started with Momma Gloria, and just got worse from there.

☠♏⌧♦

Dear Diary –

The moments I feel the weakest and those where I feel the most proud often come one after the other, if not somehow mysteriously at the same time. That is what one of the girls told me today in her session. I was struck by the eloquence of what she said, thrown forward in my chair as she spoke. I sat, beaming with joy at a woman who was never going to leave this place, a woman who would never know the joy of true freedom again, but in the space of a breath, had given me that which I couldn't express, myself. Her truth was my truth and to share it with someone touched my soul. If only I could have shared my joy with her, the circle would have been complete.

But that isn't the role of the counselor. It isn't what I'm here to do. I don't profess to know anything more about the passions of these criminals and mothers and artists than I allow them to know about me.

"The process of saving souls, Sister," I was told by Father Tervis, "does not rely on your ability to connect with those to whom you minister. God touches each soul independently, knowing when and where and why they need Him. We are His servants, shepherding the weak and sinister to Him such that He may render divine salvation for them when He chooses."

That might have been the day, more than three decades ago, where I felt my spirit begin to wither. Father Tervis stood, waited for me to stand and acknowledge his departure, and walked out.

Why, I wondered, had God not divined that the time was nigh for my own salvation? Half as old as I am today, I stood and stared at the space where Father Tervis had occupied not ten seconds previous, and wondered if I was worthy of salvation. I wondered if I had angered God so that my time was not of importance. Suffering, perhaps, would be my path toward salvation, but for how long and why? If the process of saving souls did not rely on my ability to connect with those to whom I ministered, on what then, not yet 30 years old and a devoted child of God, should I rely?

I felt very weak in that moment, standing in the void of that conversation. And at the same time I felt an overpowering sense of sinful pride in knowing that Father Tervis was wrong. Souls are the embodiment of God, of the love and life sacrificed by Jesus on the Cross. They had to be. Were they not, Jesus would have died in vain, and the world would not be what it is today. Surely Father Tervis would have understood that reasoning. To question him, his worthiness, his importance not only to the parish, but ultimately to himself, would be as destructive as anything I could imagine, so I naturally said nothing. To delight in the one-upping of someone was admittedly sinful, and I prayed for forgiveness that evening, but I also prayed that God would time my salvation soon to end my suffering.

Sitting forward in my chair, listening to the inmate try and explain herself and getting tongue-tied in the process, made me think about Janine. Her salvation was at hand. Her day of independence from the shackles of physical life would soon be here; everlasting life awaited her. I didn't mean to smile while the inmate was speaking, and she questioned me. Sinfully, or creatively, I lied and said her words had touched me. She didn't need to know I was thinking about Janine. And that was just fine with me.

June 7 (27)

Now here's what I want y'all to know about Momma Gloria. Well maybe more than just one thing. But first is I don't hold no harm against her for the way she raised me. I hate her, but I don't know how much of that is her fault. I don't know if that makes sense to y'all. In some ways, it don't make much sense to me, but I can't think of no other good way to explain it.

That day she hit me when we played the talkin game, it was like her other side came out. Momma Gloria had more than one person in her, and sometimes you got the nice one, and most of the time you got the bitch. Like when you got tore up or blamed for somethin you weren't doin, or popped in the mouth for no goddamn reason at all, that was the bitch side comin out. Sometime we wonder what Herbert used to see in her. I mean, why in the hell would you want to be with somebody like that for your whole life, let alone makin it legal and marryin the woman? She must have had some real good stuff, if you know what I mean. Haha, people gonna turn up noses when they read that. It ain't right talking about your momma like that they gonna say, but hell, what else could it have been?

I'm rememberin a lot more about Momma Gloria every day I write. Maybe that's what Sister was talkin about when she said the present makes up the past on the way to the future. One more time, that's some sneaky brainy shit Sister be tellin me as she walk out the dayroom, and it don't hit until later. I was lyin in bed thinkin about what I was gonna write, how I was gonna tell the story of my life when Sister's words popped into my head. Damn she sneaky.

Anyway, I remember more and more about Momma Gloria as I write this stuff down. I still shiver to think about her when she was mad at me. But I see little glimpses (I think that's the right word) of her when she was smilin. And she ain't smile more than when she was in the kitchen. Lord, that woman could burn with the best of them, even better at considerin how young she was, than the old women in the neighborhood. Probably coulda had her own spot if she coulda gotten a loan. But on account of her being a black woman with no business experience, and nobody to say she could do what she claimed she could – which was burn her big, black ass off – wasn't no bank gonna put up the money. Her cooking was what everybody talked about all over the neighborhood. Sometime, when somebody died or it was a holiday or somethin, Momma Gloria would make a cake or some fried chicken or maybe some chitlins if she found some that didn't stink too bad. Sometimes, she would let me help make whatever it was she was givin to whatever family was in need. We were so poor, we didn't have two nickels to rub together, but it didn't matter. That was the good side of Momma Gloria, helpin other people. Hell, it might have been the side she showed Herbert before he put her in the bed. Bet that son of a bitch wished he coulda seen into the future! Haha!

I didn't much care for her when she had me in her sights, and I would try my damnedest to not be around when she was mad. She wasn't like that with Shaniqua. Ever. She could break a plate or cuss or not do chores, and Momma Gloria wouldn't be near as hard on her as me. It took a long time for me to figure out just why it was she hated me so much most of the time. I think it comes down to me ruinin her life. Which, if you think about it, wasn't my damn fault anyway, cause I ain't the one who raped the bitch in the first place. But you can't tell her that. Nope. And trust me, we already had that conversation – it was more like a one-sided screaming match, really – but she knew how I felt about her and that lowly son of a bitch out there who is my daddy. Don't worry. I'ma get to that part, too.

I remember I cussed her on her deathbed, told her everything on my mind, screamin and spittin before we got separated. She was cryin, but probably just cause she couldn't get up and hit my ass.

Woman been dead and gone I don't know how long and she still make me feel some kinda way when I think about her. Ain't that some shit?

But I don't want to go there yet. I ain't tryin to get ahead of myself. See how easy she makes me get off track? It was like that for a long time, and started when I was a really little girl.

She used to call me Puddin. As I got older, round 4 is when I know for sure she called me that, but she coulda been calling me that since I was a baby. She called me Puddin and not my government name. And I hated it. She ain't call me Puddin cause I liked it, or cause she liked it. She called me Puddin cause it reminded her of Latta's chocolate puddin. Latta May is my grandmomma in case I ain't said that before. Latta I hear tell was a big old girl and probably where Momma Gloria learned to burn. And Latta loved her big ass some puddin. It was lumpy and real dark and bitter to the taste. Latta also loved her some dark chocolate, so she made puddin taste the way she liked it, everybody else be damned. Momma Gloria hated that puddin just as much she hated me, I guess. Puddin, go get my cigarettes off the table. Puddin, why you wearing my lipstick? Puddin why you ain't walk the dog like I told you to? Puddin this and Puddin that. I told myself one day she was gonna call me Puddin and I was gonna haul off and sock her in the fuckin mouth.

I was about five, I think, and she was pregnant with Shaniqua. She was big as a house, and that made smile to no end. She was always mad at the world, too, and couldn't nobody do anythin right. Herbert shoulda had that thing cut off after Shaniqua was born. Dumb ass kept puttin it to Momma Gloria.

I know where babies come from watchin Herbert sex up the next door neighbor, Mrs. Sanderson. Momma Gloria was in the kitchen, slavin away and she was goin on about somethin and she made me run across the street to Mrs. Sanderson. I think she was makin somethin cause somebody died, if memory serves, and ran out of some salt or somethin. I don't know. She'd sent Herbert over to get it from Mrs. Sanderson, but I guess he was takin too long, so she sent me after him. Now, Herbert wasn't no great catch by any stretch. He was the opposite of Momma Gloria in that he was tall and kinda skinny framed. I'm thinkin he had at least ten years on Momma Gloria. When they got together, she was needin a man, and he was needin a woman so it worked. Attraction must have come on later. Anyway, he was a red bone with a great smile and he could tell a joke like nobody's business. And he was the God's honest hardest workin man I ever knew in my life. But he liked to talk. Momma Gloria said he liked to talk the pants off ladies. But at five, you don't know what adults are talkin about. Me, hell I was just tryin to make the time between whippins as spread out as possible, so I did whatever Momma Gloria said.

I walked right on across the street and into Mrs. Sanderson's house. I always did that. She never locked a door, and she didn't have no children and she liked my company. It was a place I could go when Momma Gloria was on a rampage. Mrs. Sanderson always tried best she could and to keep me safe.

I didn't see or hear nobody in the kitchen, so I walked upstairs. Momma Gloria said it wasn't right to steal from nobody (which is gonna be a trip for y'all later on), so before I took whatever it was I'd been sent over to get, I wanted to make sure Mrs. Sanderson knew what I was takin. I got to the top of the stairs and I heard a bunch of moanin. Sounded like Herbert after he cut the grass, all pitiful and tired. I looked through the railin when I got to the top of the stairs and looked into Mrs. Sanderson's bedroom and I saw her bent over a table or desk, her skirt up over her waist, and Herbert standin behind her. His big old thing was goin back and forth, inside and outside Mrs. Sanderson. I heard her say, don't you put no baby in me Herbert, like you done to Gloria. He kept on moaning and she kept on bending over. I'd heard some of the older kids talkin about relations once, and even though I wasn't sure what relations were, from the way they were whisperin and snickerin about, I figured that seemed pretty close. And since Momma Gloria had a baby in her, and that's what Mrs. Sanderson didn't want, I figured I was right on the money the way I was thinkin.

I slinked back down the stairs tryin to be as quiet as a church mouse, got a cup full of sugar – that's what it was! I was after sugar the whole time – I got me a cup of sugar, and skipped back across the street to mean old Momma Gloria. I was pretty sure Herbert wasn't supposed to be puttin his big old thing inside and outside Mrs. Sanderson, and it made me smile knowin how he was gettin over on that witch. I set the sugar down and smiled. The hell you smilin about Puddin she ask me. I just shook my head, watched her measure out some salt and then the sugar into a bowl and kept it movin.

The more I sit and think about it now, the more I recall about that day. It ain't clear, but memories don't have to be clear to hit you the right way. Shaniqua has no idea why she don't like sweet stuff, but I do. Momma Gloria, for years after that, wondered why Herbert volunteered to cut Mrs. Sanderson's grass when she could have just as damn easily done it herself. And I always wondered why I not only like to cook for anybody who'll eat it, but I may or may not be prone to flyin off the handle, too. Life is crazy, ain't it?

☠♏☒♦

I got a lot on my mind tonight. Shit happens like that sometimes. I got more to say. Better get it out now before they kill me, right?

I'm pretty sure I told y'all that Momma Gloria was a little thing before she got raped. Maybe I did, and maybe I didn't. But she was. She had the world before her in a way. Cute and sexy little things like her were prime pickins for men of a certain age who wanted a trophy wife, somebody they could keep up and show off to friends and strangers. She was a confident thing, the way Herbert used to tell it, not afraid of speakin her mind and puttin herself in a position to get what she wanted. Herbert knew Momma Gloria before she got attacked so he knows both sides of her.

She was nineteen or twenty when she got attacked. After she got raped, no man would have anythin to do with her. And that's bullshit cause it wasn't her fault. She didn't ask for nothin like that to happen. It just did. But to hear Herbert tell it, you'd have thought she was tainted or some shit. Like touchin her or bein seen with her in public would get you talked about. And let me just tell you somethin. Bitches back in the day threw shade like champs. Bitches today ain't got nothin on bitches back in the day. They was flyin up one side and down the other on anybody who walked by with a past – most of it twisted from truth to lies. Bitches talked about Momma Gloria so bad once, I was told Latta beat two of them down in the street as a lesson to the other bitches. Message sent, but she still wasn't gettin a man and especially not with a baby – me – she had as a result of gettin raped.

I got off topic. Again.

Shaniqua don't like sweet things or nothin with sugar, Herbert liked cuttin more than grass, and Momma Gloria started wonderin why people pushed her away. Everybody but me, that is, until I couldn't take it no more. I am a grown ass woman, and I'm haunted by my dead momma. I'm just like her. I'm dark, I have a shape to me some people might call curves, but I'm just a woman is all. I'm tall like I said, but that's gotta come from my real daddy. Remember just like Diana Ross in The Wiz, but after I ate the scarecrow. Now that's funny, child.

I had good hair until I cut it all off. Bitches in prison gotta make do with whatever is low maintenance, like this natural. I have a stride to my walk (that Maya Angelou poem is my favorite on this earth!) like Momma Gloria, and I cuss you a blue streak when I have to. I used to smile a lot more than I do now. I've known the love of a good man (my babies daddy), and some shitty men, and I've put these curves all over some fine men I probably should have steered clear of. I've got girls who don't know me anymore, and don't know I'd die for them over and over to save them from this life. And I could burn with the best of them. Momma Gloria didn't know, or maybe she didn't care, but when she wasn't givin me down the road, I watched her. I paid attention to how she did everythin, especially cookin. Some things about Momma Gloria I ain't want to copy. Some things made me what I am today. And one of those things got my ass put on death row.

I'm just like Momma Gloria in more ways than one.

That's why I hate her. And always will.

Dear Diary –

I can't believe they are going to kill her. I know she is on death row, and I know that she is to pay for the horrible things she did to that man and woman. But I'm struggling with all of this, quite honestly. I struggle with how God is going to let one of His children die. I see it every day, on the news, in magazines; the suffering I see happening all over the world leaves me pause. How is it possible? Could any of this truly be His plan? Why can't He change the plan?

This isn't something I've told her, let alone anyone else other than God, but I feel like I'm losing my way, perhaps continuing to lose my way, having started down this path thirty years prior. I don't feel challenged by the spirit. I don't feel full of grace and light and the desire to spread the gospel. I don't know if God even cares about me anymore. The first time I saw Amethyst Janine Montgomery-Branch, I think I fell in love. And to those who would stoop to put that into an amoral context, I have to explain.

The first time I laid eyes on her was at her first trial – a preliminary hearing or arraignment, whatever it was – maybe forty years ago. I was in my early 20s and she about the same, perhaps several years younger, fifteen or sixteen, I can't be sure. We're both quite long in the tooth by now.

The judge called her name and she turned, somewhat startled either at the volume with which he said it, or the booming voice he used to speak over the noise of the gallery. He said, "Ma'am, I'm Judge Joseph Carter, and you're in my court room." She looked at her lawyer, some wet behind the ears public defender who rifled through his briefcase for that mysterious piece of paper upon which I'd assumed he had written instructions on how he should conduct himself in court. He was clueless, and that is being generous. My heart broke because I knew there was no way in the world she would receive the kind of representation she needed. I sat in a pew a few rows back from the defense table.

"Ms. Montgomery-Branch, do you know what it is you're being charged with?" She looked at Mr. Fumbles, waiting for him to say something. She'd been instructed by him not to speak, apparently. One too many television police shows under his belt, and not enough courtroom experience. When he said nothing, Janine looked at the judge and shrugged.

"You beat up your daddy, and pretty bad from what I'm told. You are charged with felony assault."

"Herbert ain't my real daddy. That's how come my last name is Montgomery-Branch. Montgomery is Momma Gloria's maiden name. Branch is her married name." Janine shot a look at her attorney who, once again, did nothing to help her in any way.

"Regardless, you were arrested, and you're now standing before me. How do you plead?" He looked over the tops of his glasses at her. I felt sick to my stomach because he wasn't looking at her as though she were a person. His gaze was tempered with indignation and irritation. The judge was doing a very poor job of hiding the dissolution of his love for the law; similar to my own walk with the Lord, the passion that had brought him to the bench seemed to wane with the rise and fall of his breath. Staring at Janine and waiting for her to say whatever it was he was waiting for her to say seemed like a stop in time he neither anticipated nor appreciated. All day long, I imagine, he sat there looking over the tops of his glasses, waiting for criminals and soccer moms and whomever else to tell them how they were going to plead, or how their attorney felt they should plead, mark down something in their file, hand it to the bailiff and move on to the next alleged criminal. "Ma'am, I ask again. How do you plead?"

I don't recall exactly how she put it, but suffice it to say that her pleading guilty was done in a manner that broke up the gallery, and in what may have been a miracle from God, even made that crusty judge crack a smile. That, I told myself, was something I should never forget.

As they escorted Janine away, presumably back to wherever they were holding her, or transporting her back to her jail cell, I felt called to service: that woman needed help, and I was the person to help her. I sat there in that courtroom, in that pew, in my starched habit and black dress, listening to the stories and lies and the creative ways men and women attempted to profess their innocence. As each person stepped forward, accompanied by counsel much stronger than the newbie standing with Janine, their pain touched me.

These were broken people, screaming out for help. I was particularly drawn to the women, imagining the horrors of surviving an abusive spouse, or doing unimaginable things to pay for the drugs to feed their addiction, or even those who harmed their children in one way or another. I knew in my soul that they were all guilty. But none of them were beyond repair. None of them were beyond the love and compassion of a merciful God, and the nurturing hand of someone who would truly care for them. I was determined to be that person. I had to start somewhere, with someone who cried out for me whether they knew it or not. Of the thirty or so people that went before Judge Carter, Amethyst Janine Montgomery-Branch had been the one and only person to plead guilty. She was the only one who told the truth.

And with her my new walk would begin.

June 8 (26)

I saw Sister today, and she had that look on her face again. She asked me what did I write since the day before and I told her nothin. That was a lie, but I don't know why she thinks it's her damn business to know everythin I do. She gave me that look and, like I always damn do, told her what I really did. Low and damn behold, she smiled. Good, Janine. The more you write, the more people gonna know the real you. I asked her why she isn't also writin. And then I answered my own question. Because they ain't gonna kill her. She got time to get her story straight. Sister might be old like me, but she got all the time in the world. Hell, she got time to make up a new story, burn the old one, and start fresh.

Ha. That's some bullshit Shaniqua used to hear when somethin went wrong. Start fresh. Fuck you, Momma Gloria, for not sayin that shit to me. I mess up and all hell breaks loose. Shaniqua does some stupid shit and she get a peppy talk.

I learned real early on that things probably wouldn't never change for me. I felt like that little bitch Cinderella, but without the slipper, and sho nuff without the prince swoopin in to marry her and take her away from that horrible step mother and those nasty ass step sisters. Nope, I was stuck with what I got. I tried to make the best of it when I wasn't mad or cryin. Truth be told, I'm glad Herbert and Momma Gloria had Shaniqua. Baby girl took the heat off of me when she was born, and I could ride under the radar and do me for a change. Shaniqua don't look or act nothin like me. She's pretty and she's real smart. Wouldn't shock me a bit to learn she wasn't Herbert's flesh and blood. Rich as all hell now, wouldn't surprise me none if she forgot she even had a sister. Without no parents and no siblings in your business, make it awful easy to reinvent yourself, don't it? But, whatever. My circumstance ain't fittin to change, so no reason to piss on what she got by reachin out before I die. Alls that's gonna do is bring up shit nobody want bringin up.

Shaniqua is five years under me, and was a bitch on wheels when she wanted to be, just like her momma. Hell, just like me, too, I guess. I was held back once or twice in primary school, so she caught up to me kinda fast. We knew the same kids, but she was a lot more popular than me. She never got in no fights at school. She said it was barbaric or somethin. But even though that little bitch was evil as hell, and didn't think she should be fightin when bitches made her mad, she ain't have no problem tellin me when somebody did her wrong.

I fought more little tramps, and even a couple of dudes who did her wrong or pissed her off. And I loved it! Made me feel important for once. Made me feel like I was somebody. She needed and depended on me and came to me when she needed help. I ain't never got the feelin from Momma Gloria or Herbert or just about nobody else that they needed me. And even if I was only boppin some tramp on the skull or puttin my finger in some boy's face, I was there for Shaniqua and she knew it. Hell, if you look at it funny, maybe I was her damn knight in shiny armor. Ain't that some shit? Ha Ha.

9 times out of 10, I could mix it up with whoever, walk away and never get in trouble. And let me tell you Shaniqua been causin trouble and gettin me into tight spots since she was knee-high. I think the first time I had to beat a bitch down, the child was three or four, so that'd made me eight or nine. Shaniqua is lighter than me, kinda like some strawberry milk chocolate, where I'm just as dark as Hershey's. Momma Gloria ain't no darker than me or anybody else, and Herbert is about as red bone as it gets.

I had to look up to see what I was talking about before I got off track. Like I said, the first time I had to beat a bitch down was when I was eight or nine. Somebody said somethin stupid to Shaniqua. I think maybe they said she was actin white or somethin like that. Shaniqua always had good teeth and some good hair, and she liked to wear pretty things. Momma Gloria would spend a little extra on her baby, so she was absolutely a spoiled brat. I had some good hair, too, but we was a long way off from goin to the hair dresser once a week like some bitches I know did before they got locked up. We made do is what I'm tryin to say. Well, somebody said whatever they said to little miss actin white and she came home cryin. Momma Gloria was in a mood, and to my complete surprise, apparently she told Shaniqua to stop her goddamn cryin. Herbert wasn't nowhere to be found, so she came to me.

Lookin back on it now, I know it was a bad idea to do what I did. But when I finally found her and had her on the ground, I felt like a god. Patty somethin or other. God that was a long ass time ago. Patty Stringfield, maybe. If she's livin, she's gonna be pissed I wrote about her in this thing. I love that, too. Anyway, Shaniqua came and got me from the house and went lookin for Patty. Found her on the playground outside our neighborhood. She turned Michael Jackson white when she saw me comin, with Shaniqua frilly little ass stompin right behind me. I jerked her little ass down from the swings and sat on top of her. I slapped her a couple of times in the face and told her that she wasn't never to mess with Shaniqua or think about sayin some stupid shit about her ever again. I cocked my hand up real high in the air and asked her did she understand my damn words. She said yes and I let her up. I snatched her ass by the hair when she tried to run away and told her that if anybody ever found out I'd kill her with my bare hands. I don't know if she'd wet herself or if I'd put her in a puddle on the ground, but you could see the wet spot on her rear as she ran home. Shaniqua and I just died laughin.

Momma Gloria never found out. Patty kept her damn mouth shut and she lived to see another day. And Shaniqua knew that nobody would ever mess with her again.

Sister asked me every now and then about my family and I never wanted to say nothin about them. Somehow, some way, they all let me down, or left me driftin on my own when all I needed might have been just a damn helpin hand. Shit, I'd just taken a shoulder if they'd give it to me. I asked Sister if she had anybody like that and she said me. Bitch tryin to make me cry. I asked why me and she said somethin about the first day she ever saw me or heard me. She knew that I was somethin and somebody special and that she needed to know me. That was a long ass time ago when I got locked up in South Carolina and she just appeared out of nowhere. These days that shit's called stalkin and you can arrested for it. HaHa!

She sat and told me everythin she could remember about that first day. I'd put it out of my mind if I'm being honest. One of the worst days of my life never seemed to end for days and weeks and months. I didn't want to think about it anymore, and it's the one damn thing she holds onto because it brought me into her life. I know she's gonna say explain it, and so I don't have to hear her mouth, here it is.

I was seventeen, shit maybe even sixteen, I'm not sure. Shaniqua was comin off the school bus and I was walkin down to get her, like I usually did. Momma Gloria ain't want her walkin back to the house unescorted, but she had no problem with my ass walkin by myself. Stupid. Anyhow, after I got her from the stop, we turned and started back up the hill to the house. I looked up and saw Momma Gloria runnin across the street into Mrs. Sanderson's house. And then I saw Mrs. Sanderson, Herbert and Momma Gloria all runnin out of Mrs. Sanderson's house at the same time, one after the other like a Tom & Jerry cartoon.

Momma Gloria looked like she had a knife or somethin shiny in her hand. Mrs. Sanderson was screamin like a stuck pig, and darted to the left. I stopped dead in my tracks and watched the whole thing. Momma Gloria got up to Herbert and threw whatever it was she had in her hands at him, and his ass stopped dead in his tracks, too. They was yellin and screamin and cussin each other. Herbert had his work shirt in one hand, and he was pullin up his braces over his undershirt with the other. Must have been puttin that big old thing in a bent over Mrs. Sanderson again, and Momma Gloria either found out, or she'd just damn had enough.

I sent Shaniqua to a friend just below our house, but it didn't do no good. If I didn't want her to see the fight, it didn't matter because everybody and they momma had come outside to see what the hell was happenin. I started runnin when I saw Herbert ball up his fist and hit Momma Gloria dead in her face. She dropped like a wet sock.

Oh hell no, I said. You ain't fittin to be puttin your hands on my momma like that! I still remember every word I said. Momma Gloria's nose was bleedin and she tried coverin up because Herbert was windin up for another shot, gonna hit her on the ground. I jumped his ass and let my weight bring him to the ground, him on his back and me tryin to straddle him. Now Herbert wasn't no munchkin. I know he stood six feet somethin, about four inches taller than me. And he might have weighed a little more, but you can't do nothin against a bitch on fire.

You want to hit my momma like she a man? I was screamin. I reared back and cocked that son of a bitch in the nose and it busted like a vase. I hit him three or four times in a row real quick before he lifted a leg and kneed me in the crotch. Now listen here girls. I don't know about a man's balls, and I've kicked many a guy in the nuts, but don't nothin hurt like when a girl gets kicked in the lady bits. I just about blacked out. He stood up, massagin his face and put his shirt up to his nose to catch the blood. I looked over and Momma Gloria had propped up on her knees, and was cryin for us to stop. Herbert told her to shut the ever livin fuck up and I lost it again.

I knew it was a knife Momma Gloria chased them with because I saw it at the steps. She must have threw it at him and probably seein the knife fly by him is what made him turn around. He ain't have to punch her like that, and he was gonna pay for it.

He told my momma to shut the ever livin fuck up again because she just kept on damn cryin and I went for the knife. He saw me on the side of his face and liked to take off runnin. He slipped in the grass and I was on him. I threw a knee into his ribs and jabbed the handle of the knife into his neck. Wasn't no way I was gonna kill him. That thought ain't even cross my mind. I really did love Herbert, but he needed to know he wasn't gonna just do that shit to Momma Gloria and get away with it. I don't give a damn about what he wanted to do with Mrs. Sanderson, but ain't no hands goin on Momma Gloria like that. Push her around was one thing, but bustin somebody nose wasn't no joke, and wasn't no shit I was about to stand for. Like I said, I wasn't gonna kill him. He just needed to be scared of me. I popped him again one good time in the face, the handle of the knife taking up every bit of empty space in my fist.

I heard sirens comin and was about to hit him one more time when Momma Gloria knocked me off him and to the ground. Bitch must have took a runnin start and tackled my ass. You forgot she thick until she hits you like she did me. Don't kill him, she kept screamin. Don't kill him. I still shake my head when I hear that. Don't kill him. Why was she chasin him with a knife out of Mrs. Sanderson's? Wasn't like she just wanted to scare him. And she threw the son of a bitch at him while he was runnin away. Don't kill him. Say what?! Bitch, please.

Next thing I know, boom, I'm gettin arrested, and Momma Gloria ain't say a thing to the police about Herbert bustin her in the face. And then, boom, I'm standin next to a first-year public defender who don't know shit about shit. And then, boom, I get handed six years for felony assault. On a first goddam offense. That was my first strike.

You're welcome, Momma Gloria.

Sister was there in court the day I got sentenced, too. She sat quiet and watched the whole thing unfold. Watched me get skewered. And except for about six years once, she ain't hardly ever been out of my life since.

☠♏☒♦

Dear Diary –

There is something oddly comforting about being alone, about being adrift by yourself in the middle of something so titanic and immeasurable with the naked eye. To find a way to be at peace with yourself, given the chaos which swirls around you, is a skill and a blessing of talent from God. That's what I said this morning to a young prisoner I'll call Sonya. I have decided against using her given name for the sake of her privacy, and that's probably best for all involved.

She came into my office today for her normal appointment. We were going to talk about the progress she's made in her fight against herself and her inability to accept where she is. We were going to talk about how proud I am of her for becoming her own person, leaving behind the timid pushover who arrived three months ago on a prison bus from God knows where. We were going to talk about her blossoming and her decision to stand up for herself when challenged and her starting to feel large in a space so small. But we didn't. We didn't touch on any of that. She walked into my office today for her normal appointment and she cursed at me.

Fuck God, she spat, sitting down in a lumpy mess in the chair facing my desk. I'm honestly not quite sure what she expected me to say. It certainly wasn't the response she had imagined. Yes, I said. Fuck God. Sonya's eyes lit up and then darkened instantly as she peered at me through tiny slits, untrusting and suspicious. She accused me of making fun of her and stood to leave. I'm out of here, she screamed.

I'm 65 years old, I started. She stood there with her hand on the door knob. We both knew she wasn't going anywhere. I'm 65 years old, I'm alone and without a husband. I'm 65 years old and I have chosen to surround myself with criminals and psychopaths. I'm 65 years old and too frumpy to attract or maintain a boyfriend. I'm 65 years old and I haven't been a nun in the eyes of God or the Holy See since I was 25. Yet I'm here, I speak the truths of the gospel and of life because I believe this is where God has led me; this is where I do His work under the governance of His word and deed. I'm 65 years old and the greatest joy in my life is serving you. Fuck God.

She sat down.

We stared at one another for a moment, neither of us probably sure of what we should say next. She licked her lips and looked around the room. So tell me why you aren't a nun.

Very nearly 40 years ago, I began, my life seemed to dissolve before me. Ten years before that, tender and dangerously innocent at 15, I almost died. She sat forward in her chair, more intrigued in my story with every word.

When I was 14 years old, I lived a pretty comfortable life. I went to private school, I had parents who never once thought about beating me, I had every imaginable pleasure, I enjoyed privilege and I took it for granted. As a way to impress a boy, I smoked my first joint, and then some short weeks later, I sniffed cocaine. Several months after that, around my 15th birthday party, I shot heroin for the first time. I nicknamed it Brad so I could talk about him in front of my parents without them catching on. And we instantly fell in love with each other. He was a little harder on me than I was on him, of course, but every time we were together – which became more and more often – the feelings got stronger and stronger. I needed Brad. And he knew it.

I felt my elbow itch and wondered if I should be talking about this with her. Unethical is an understatement. I ignored the itch and continued. She was still rapt. Her file told me she would be.

One day, Brad got a little aggressive. Truth was, I egged him on. I'd told him I wasn't afraid of him. I told him that he could do whatever he wanted to me and I'd still love him. My friends told me Brad was hurting me, that he was pulling me down. I was suffering in school, I was more and more withdrawn and I was very argumentative with my parents. I had a secret, though, something I shared with my mother, but something I didn't dare tell anyone, so I kept my mouth shut and saw Brad more often than I should have. My friends were scared for me. They told me that I should leave Brad and get help. But I wasn't listening to them – or myself. I loved Brad and that was that.

The day Brad went farther than I wanted him to was the day I almost died. I'd snuck out of school, Brad tucked discreetly into my satchel and set off for home. I don't know why, probably because we knew my mother would be home when we arrived, but we didn't want to wait until we got home and I stopped behind an old building on the grounds of my church just outside my neighborhood to get a fix. Can you just picture a little girl all of 15 in her Catholic school uniform, squatting between a dumpster and the abandoned church building only shouting distance from the cathedral where she takes mass, spoon in hand and lighter underneath, waiting for Brad to do his worst? My parents never looked at my feet, which meant the webbing between my toes was the best place for the needle. I could slip my Mary Janes on and off with ease, even when the anticipation was more than I could manage.

Brad took me down that day.

I didn't know how long I'd been in the abandoned building. I didn't know how many times I'd been raped. Or by whom. I didn't know why I was bleeding or why my priest was praying over me or why my mother was in tears in an ambulance racing at the speed of light to the hospital. I didn't know why Brad was doing any of those horrible things to me and making me vomit on myself. I didn't know why even after I was discharged and sent to rehab that I went back to Brad. I didn't know then why my parents kicked me out after I sold some things for Brad. I didn't know who I was or where I was going. Until the day God found me again and took me into His heart.

Sonya had started crying not out of compassion for me, but because my story was so much like her own.

My passion for Him so easily replaced my passion and desire and lust for Brad. It was though Brad never existed and the high I had been looking for was the Holy word. I graduated from high school, I started in seminary school, and I'd pledged my life in all forms and endeavors to lifting up His name.

And? And, she said.

And then some years later, Brad found me again.

Yes, there is something comforting about being alone, about being adrift. But comfort is often found in the arms and smiles and hands of those around you; people who care for you and want only the best for you. And that comfort is returned when you extend the same love to someone else. I would be adrift were it not for Janine. He brought both Brad and Janine into my life, each a drug of their own kind. And even though I'm not sure if he cares, I thank God for her every day.

June 9 (25)

You hear people say that you don't really know what you don't have until it's gone, right? Well, that ain't always the case, especially in the hood. I take that back. We didn't really live in the hood, not like you'd probably think about it today, but it was more like a whole bunch of black folks with no money, all livin together in the same neighborhood. If you're shakin your head and trying to figure out the difference between them, I'll just say that the hood was a scary place full of pimps and drug dealers and all that shit you see on TV that supposed to represent black people. But the place where I grew up wasn't nothin like that. We was just broke as is all. But we didn't know it. It didn't turn hood until later.

Other than Shaniqua getting whatever in the fuck she wanted, most of the time we did without. We didn't have no fancy clothes except around Easter. We ain't have a car that worked all the time. What we did have, unlike most of my friends was a father that worked all the time. We ain't have extra money for sweet treats or pop or gum. Momma Gloria made clothes and food from scratch, kept the house, and we just had what we needed and got along fine.

When you don't have nothin and nobody around you got shit, neither, everybody is the same. Yes, most everybody had a television of one way or another, but nothin special. The community where I grew up, where Momma Gloria and Herbert decided to raise two children was special in more ways than I can probably go into. I don't know how to say it right, but you had to feel it to know what I'm gettin at. It ain't somethin that was in the air or a silly thing like that. But it was more like everybody was family and took care of everybody else's everything. I'm talkin about the days when you really could beat down somebody else's kid for fuckin up. Not the it takes a village kind of bullshit people talk about now where everybody scared to lay a hand on a child or curse one of them monsters out for fear of gettin arrested. Wasn't nothin like that. Everybody looked after everybody. Well, everybody black looked after everybody else black. White folks couldn't be trusted. At least that's what I was taught when I was little.

When I was five, about the time Shaniqua was born, Herbert had him a good job. He worked in a factory puttin furniture together. I don't think he made the parts, but he is the one that glued or screwed or stapled everything together to make a chair or sofa or whatever it was he was makin that day. He was talented as all hell, but it wasn't somethin he was allowed to show at work. He made little stuff around the house with scraps he snuck back from the factory. I remember not too long before she was born, Herbert made me a doll house out of some old balsa wood he got. I didn't even have no dolls at the time. But he wanted me to have that goddam doll house. He said my baby girl gonna have this because I want her to. Hold on. It used to drive Momma Gloria out of her head when he called me baby girl. I wasn't even his, but for a long time he loved me like I was. He loved me probably more than Momma Gloria. Maybe that's what pissed her off.

Anyway, he said that every house is empty at some point. Just gonna take a little work to get somebody to move into it.

I loved that doll house so much. It wasn't the only thing that Herbert made me, but it was the closest to my heart. Momma Gloria hated it. Or maybe she just hated that Herbert wasn't treatin me like a piece of trash, that maybe he loved me and wanted to make me smile. Granted he could be a real son of a bitch to everybody in the house, especially Momma Gloria, and sure enough when he'd been out drinkin. But he had a nice soft side that wandered out every now and then to say hi.

That soft side made a doll house, empty as all hell, but it was mine. And I loved Herbert for it.

Well, I don't know how much money Herbert made puttin together furniture for that company, but it wasn't enough for us to have a damn thing extra past what Shaniqua got. The mortgage, the light bill, the constant car repair, the liquor, and whatever he gave Momma Gloria damn near tapped him out every week he got his check. What little bit he had left, I found out, he squirreled away out of sight of Momma Gloria because he knew if she knew about that money, she'd have a holy fit until he turned it over to her. It was his, he earned it, and he was gonna do whatever he wanted to with it. He ain't ask her what she did with the money he gave her even though it was clear Shaniqua was suckin it up in whatever she could get out of Momma Gloria, so he didn't figure she had any right to his. But, it was safer to keep it on the low just the same.

Well, not too long before Shaniqua came beltin and screamin into the world, I must have been stompin around like a jealous lover. Momma Gloria tore me up every time the notion hit her. I swear that bitch got stronger and meaner when she was pregnant. Now she beatin me for no reason, and that hurt me in more ways than I can tell, but because Shaniqua wasn't born yet, that also meant I wasn't sharin her. Twisted, I know, but it's how it was back then. Momma Gloria was all I'd had for a long time. We was alone with each other until I was two or three, and then Herbert came back into her life. I was happy as hell to have a daddy, but it also meant I'd only have half of a momma. That hurt the most on days when she was lovin towards me. It still hurts, really.

Anyway, right before Shaniqua the Great was born, I moped around not wantin to share my space or room or food or momma or air with nobody, and H to the no did I want to share it with somebody who was gonna be cryin and shittin and screamin all day long. So to cheer me up, Herbert took out some of his sock money and we snuck down to Draper's to buy me a dolly or two, because my real house was gonna fill up, and Herbert said he figured my dolly house should, too.

Momma Gloria was taking a nap and just before she fell out, Herbert said he was gonna take me for a walk. She said don't you let Puddin get you in no trouble. She's bad for that. And she was out like a light. I don't know why I was bad for gettin nobody in trouble. And, besides, Herbert was a grown ass man. Even I knew he could handle himself.

Remember, I'm five or somethin like that. A child.

When we got to Draper's, we waited until it was clear and we walked in. Draper's catered to the white crowd, and even in the day and age when any black person was supposed to by law be able to go into any store they wanted, different rules applied to folks in the south and Charlotte wasn't no different. And knowin your place made sure you lived to see another day. I still cringe when I think about how they did Emmett Till like that for whistlin at a white girl. But that's what was on the mind of a black man, in the south, for a long time after it happened. Somethin like that never really leaves the mind. How can it?

Well, we walked into Draper's and Herbert nodded real polite at the man behind the counter and we walked to the sewin section. Herbert pointed at a dolly and smacked my hand real loud as I reached out to touch it. Don't never touch nothin that ain't belong to you, Janine. He never called me Puddin in his life. Don't never touch nothin he said. You gonna pay for it, that's one thing, but handlin somethin that ain't yours will get you beat down. He looked at me kind of like he wanted to know did what he say sink in, and the other part was kind of sorry for having to smack me and tell me what he did. I pointed at the dolly I wanted and Herbert walked to the counter and paid.

The clerk didn't touch Herbert. Herbert put the money on the counter and nodded. Some white folks came in the store and the clerk tightened up a little bit like he'd been caught doing somethin he wasn't supposed to. Herbert got a little tight, too, but I didn't know why. So I started talkin. He's gonna buy me that dolly so I can put it in the doll house he made me. He's real good at makin stuff. Herbert put his hand on my shoulder to try and quiet me down. I just kept talkin. I didn't understand the shoulder trick. Just tell me what you want and I'll do it. Too late.

My Herbert made this doll house for me, I said. He used wood he got from work and he painted it and said that some houses need dollys and now I'm gettin a dolly.

Small town at the time, well at least in that part of Charlotte if that makes sense, so that meant most everybody knew who Herbert was, and where he worked. And whoever that other white guy was who walked in when we paid must have gotten the wrong idea about Herbert and my dolly house and the wood he used to make it. We paid real quick and Herbert snatched me up and left fast. I was playin with my new dolly all the way back to the house and didn't pay attention to Herbert not sayin anythin. I was in my own little world, happy as a fist full of clams about my dolly. Her name was Eva.

That was a Saturday. Shaniqua was born on Tuesday. Herbert got called into his boss's office on Wednesday and got fired. They said he was stealin wood he wasn't entitled to have. That's where my dolly house came from. That tappin on my shoulder was meant for me to shut up. It meant for me to stop talkin, and said you're gonna get me in trouble. Herbert saw the white man walk into Draper's. That's why he tightened up like the clerk did. That white guy went and told what he heard, Herbert lost his job, right when we had another mouth to feed, and me and my dolly didn't know nothin about nothin.

One more thing for Momma Gloria to put on my shoulders. One more thing for her to hate me for.

Well, what I was talkin about in the beginnin was not knowin what you ain't got until you ain't got it. Not too long after that all happened, I realized what people meant when they said it. Momma Gloria naturally blamed me for Herbert losin his job. And I agreed with her. Children shouldn't never think about killin themself, and I'm kinda ashamed to admit it, but the thought crossed my mind, even when I was so young. If I knew how to do it back then, I might have. I hurt so bad that I let Herbert and even Momma Gloria down. I wanted to be dead and gone. I ain't never told nobody that – never even told Sister. I hope she won't be mad at me when she reads this. Herbert losin his job and Momma Gloria beatin me for it was the very first time – and not the last time since – I wished I'd never been born.

☠♏⌧♦

Dear Diary –

There was a pain, unspecific and unbridled, in Janine's eyes during today's session. It was biting, even as an outsider looking in, and I dare say that it has left an indelible mark upon me that I wasn't expecting.

I have become quite accustomed to Janine's personality over these last forty or so years, in and out of correctional facilities, in and out of my life and direct line of counseling. I know when she's hurting. And I know what makes her sad. I sat today and looked at her for as many moments as she would allow before breaking my gaze and beginning our conversation with a jab. That is the Janine I know who is in pain, who is shutting down, who is in emotional peril. I asked her what it was she had written lately, thinking that she would be agreeable to talking about that, as opposed to whatever it was that had diminished her mood, looming death sentence, notwithstanding.

She took a long, deliberate breath, avoiding looking at me directly and exhaled. Still not looking at me, she said my children will never again know me as their momma. They won't even know I'm dead until they get the next of kin letter. And that's if they read it. I don't have no part of their lives, and it don't hurt them.

I stood and walked to her, sitting next to her at the table in the dayroom. I looked back at Martinez, the guard who accompanied Janine to this session and she nodded, compassion flowing through her, knowing what I needed to do.

Very gently, I took Janine's hands in my own, and together we cried.

June 10 (24)

The problem growin up poor is that you don't have nobody who expects shit from you. I don't know if that makes sense to people who ain't come from the hood or don't know nobody from the hood. Once you're born into the hood, or somehow you find your way into the hood, it's like you trapped there for life. Either you gonna die there, you get thrown in jail for some shit you did in the hood, or you beat the odds and find a way to get the fuck out. And that don't happen a lot. I mean, shit, look at TV and the news and you can see that. Born and die in the hood. That's the way it's supposed to be, I guess.

We didn't live in the 'hood' when we came up. I told y'all that already. We were poor, yeah, but it wasn't like we had anythin less than our friends. Yeah, we knew white folks and uppity black folks who ain't live in the hood had it good, but it wasn't like we knew better than what we had. Some folks lost they house when times got bad, but we got everything we have from that place, and it will always be home.

You see, wasn't no drugs and gang killin in the old days when I was comin up. People used to beef, that's no doubt. But wasn't nobody pullin straps on brothers and bitches wasn't cuttin bitches with razors in they mouths. I used to be nice with my hands, and everybody knew it. Shaniqua got herself in a jam, like I said before, and I was there to settle motherfuckers down and put my hands on anybody who disagreed with the law – me. Everybody knew the liquor houses, and everybody damn sure knew when the first and fifteenth rolled around. But we always operated under the same idea: don't start none, won't be none.

Momma Gloria wasn't gonna stand for nobody bringin no kind of shit into her house, and she didn't care if it was me, Herbert, or the angel. Momma Gloria had skills and would have fought a bear to keep things the way she wanted in her house. Just like everybody knew I was nice with my hands, they also knew don't fuck with Momma Gloria for nothin, cause you damn sure gonna regret it.

Okay, so I'ma give you a tip. Anybody think they want to roll up into the hood out of curiosity or because you think you doin the poor folk a favor, nuh uh, forget it. We don't need you and just like the police, we probably don't trust you, neither. As time went on, and we got new generations of people on the block and surroundin, things started to change. Things got worse, people got angrier, things came up missin from porches and back yards with no dogs and shit. Crack was just startin to get a hold of people and it was startin to look like the shit was gonna get real bad before it got any better.

Five-O rolled through all the time, but not like they do in white neighborhoods when they checkin to see if them plastic bitches and Ken dolls was cool. Nope, they roll through the hood makin sure that we ain't killin nobody but ourselves. Serve and protect my ass. And you better leave that in the book when I'm dead. Police ain't do shit in the hood other than say they was there in case somebody starts shootin. Anyway, don't get me started. Police been gettin my pressure up since I was a little girl. Look at me now.

Right, so you know you're poor in the hood, you know that the only way out of the hood that you've ever seen anybody do is in a bag or handcuffs, and nobody – and I mean nobody – ever got out for doin some shit that was positive. Regina Becker was special and made the mistake of tellin her momma how much better she was and how she'd never leave her kids to grow up in filth and nothin like her and her brothers did. Me and Regina went to Olympic high school and she was a track all-star. She was about as bright as a box of weave, but bitch was a stunner on the track. She was the same age as me. I used to remember watchin her at track meets and think about how badly I wished I was fast enough to run away from the hood and Momma Gloria and my life. That bitch turnt me green every time I saw or thought about her.

Regina knew she was special. She was right about that. We were 16 at the time (this was probably two weeks before I beat down Herbert for punching Momma Gloria) and I'd heard that somebody was lookin at her to run for them in college. Now that was some shit, cause that didn't happen. College wasn't nothin we thought about because couldn't nobody afford it. I mean, it costs thousands and thousands of dollars just to go. Then you gotta pay to live and eat and whatever else you do at college. The hell with that. There was plenty of jobs in Charlotte to be had, but the game was all about assistance. Sling for somebody a little bit, pick up your check on the first and fifteenth, have a baby and another and another, and it was a wrap. Regina was about to get out. We talked about how she was gonna run for a college, and get a degree, and then maybe a good job. We was gonna stay in touch and she'd help me get out. My grades weren't good – and ain't no way I'd have got into college even if I could get a loan or a scholarship or whatever. In my mind, for no damn good reason, Regina Becker was my ticket out.

And she would have been if she'd kept her damn mouth shut.

Regina's momma was drinkin that night. She was hittin it hard and it wasn't the right time for Regina to tell her she sucked as a momma and a provider. The woman flew into a rage. Now, this is what I heard cause I wasn't there. Might be true, might not be true. But the end result is the same.

I hear she jumped up from the chair or sofa or whatever and got in Regina's face talkin about, you don't know shit about shit. And sayin that if it wasn't for her, they wouldn't have no place to stay as it is. Oh, Regina's momma was basically a prostitute. That's how she paid her rent and paid for her liquor. She used to bang men in the neighborhood, or anybody else who give her some cash to drop her panties. That, more than anything, hurt Regina most. Her momma had such little respect for herself, she ain't have no more instinct to provide for her children.

Like I said, she jumped up from the sofa or whatever and started puttin her finger in Regina's face. Well, trust and believe when I say that's some shit you didn't do to Regina Becker. I don't know if she was even thinkin straight cause Regina slapped her hand away. They said she was yellin and cussin her momma a blue streak. She put her finger in Regina's face one more gain and Regina punched her in the nose, droppin her back into the chair. Oh shit, here we go. Her momma stood up, stared at her and said somethin like that's the last time you ever gonna put hands on me. They ran around the livin room, Regina runnin from her momma and screamin. Nobody know where her sister and brothers were. They was probably too scared to come down stairs. And it ain't like it was the first time Regina and her momma had beef.

They rounded the corner one more time and Regina dipped into the kitchen. She grabbed a big ass knife from the drawer, and backed herself into the corner with the stove and the kitchen sink. Her momma grabbed one of them liquor bottles from the counter, smashed that son of a bitch across the wall, and threw it at Regina. Busted her dead in the face. She fell to the ground. The ambulance drivers and the police said in the papers that her momma must have stabbed her over 100 times, pinned there in the corner, layin in the floor. Regina died that night. Just like my dream of gettin the fuck out of there, too.

Know what Momma Gloria said when she found out? She looked me in my face and told me I'd better not be gettin full of myself like Regina. Look what happened to her, she said. We were sittin at the dinner table, at dinner, everybody watchin and listenin. Momma Gloria plain as day told me not to expect nothin out of life. You right where you always gonna be Puddin. Nobody expected nothin from me anyway, she said so I'd might as well get used to it. It was Regina's fault her mother stabbed her to death. It was Regina's fault for sayin what she did that drove the woman crazy. It was Regina's fault.

That was the night I silently decided Momma Gloria was gonna die by my hands. If she ain't chase after Herbert with a knife, ain't get popped in the face, and if I hadn't beat her husband down landin my big ass in jail, no tellin what might have happened. And Momma Gloria got to walk the earth a little bit longer.

June 11 (23)

James 1:5
"But if any of you lacks wisdom, let him ask of God, who gives to all generously and without reproach, and it will be given to him."

I read that today before anything else. I was sitting in my office, dreading the day – the dead end of my words and the futility of my actions – when I opened my Bible. James has always inspired me. This day isn't unlike any other.

Of the women that I counsel here, I know the vast majority will never walk a straight and narrow path again, regardless of their incarceration. It should pain me to see the same faces enter and leave this facility. But the truth of the matter is that I would rather they were here, with me, protected from those forces of evil outside these walls than exposed in a society which has proved to callously and viciously toss them aside when it is convenient. My struggle with the directing hand of the Almighty brings me pain and guilt at the same time. I know He is the creator and planner of and for every creature on this world and others. But that love is tested when I see these girls and wonder why He isn't helping THEM.

They truly lack wisdom – of self, of community, of age, of maternity. James tells me they should simply ask of God who will give it to them generously. Whether they are not asking, or they don't know that they should, James will guide my talks today. Through James will my girls learn to ask – and that through asking they will receive.

And live a better life through Him.

☠♏☒♦

I think I gotta start a little bit more at the beginnin. I read what I wrote so far last night and somethin's missin. I told Sister this mornin and she told me I need to be tellin everything I can damn think of. Don't leave nothin out. Don't think about not sayin somethin and shit like that. Whatever that means. She had this happy white girl look in her eyes and kept talkin about James and askin and the Bible. I nodded and kept it movin like usual.

I didn't write a thing after my session with Sister yesterday. I mean, I took notes, but nothin nobody considers permanent. I sat all day and thought about what she said what seems like so goddam long ago. Teach. Start at the beginnin. I don't think I did.

I was born and raised in Charlotte, North Carolina, y'all know that. You ain't gonna find too many people can say that. Most of the people there now came from someplace else. They don't know the city like I do. Like I used to. Shit, even that was a long time ago. I see pictures of downtown and all the buildings and all the people who work for the banks and shit and think back to what it used to look like when I was comin up. Hardly nothin is the same.

My parents are Gloria and Herbert. And I hate them. No more reason than anybody else who was done wrong by flesh, but I'ma get to that. I have one sister Shaniqua. That ain't her real name, but I call her Shaniqua because she used to be ghetto as hell. Like Momma Gloria callin me Puddin, Shaniqua don't like it one bit that I call her that. That's my right as the first-born. I do what I want. I love her I guess, but I ain't above tormentin her, either. I got more on Shaniqua later. She slick as a motherfucker, and that ain't no lie. Bitch learned how to code-switch and it was game over for real. I had another sister name Paula but she died when I was a little girl, right after Momma Gloria and Herbert got together. She's between me and Shaniqua, but don't nobody talk about her. It's like she's a secret Momma Gloria and Herbert be ashamed about or somethin. Maybe I'll see her if I get to go to Heaven if that shit's not a lie. I'ma be one pissed dead bitch if the afterlife is a joke. Trust and believe.

So, Herbert. You read what I wrote about Herbert earlier – sometimes he was good to me and sometimes he was out of his damn mind, whackin the shit out of me for no good reason other than Johnny Walker or Jack fuckin Daniels told him to. Herbert ain't my real daddy, but he was there from the time I was little, maybe two years old. That man the only daddy I ever had, really, so I take the good with the bad, or at least I used to. Momma Gloria she always said she got dealt a shitty hand, and that I was the first card in a deck stacked against her. And I know what you're thinkin. No, ain't no motherly award comin her way. Ever.

Momma Gloria was somethin else in her younger years – at least the way she'd tell it. Dancin and smokin and carryin on, she lived the good life up in New York City for a couple of years. She had some kind of piss ant job at a cleaners or somethin, waitin tables on the side at night for extra money for dresses and shit. I swear her jobs changed every damn time she told the story. Me and Shaniqua used to laugh our asses off where she couldn't hear each time she told somebody who ain't give a shit about her younger years that she was a cook or a maid or a nurse. Give me a fuckin break and just tell the damn story!

Whatever it was she did, and the pictures prove it, she made enough to be a fly little dresser. My eyes popped the first time I saw her fierce and dressed to the nines. Momma Gloria was creative and every part of her body was stacked with talent for makin, whether it was clothes or food. Herbert told me years on that Momma Gloria used to have a passion for design. Said her dream was to design clothes for those bitches on Soul Train! Bet yo last money it's gonna be a stone gas honey! That shit makes me smile every time. Go on, Don Cornelius. Damn! Anyway, ain't nobody brown be in the spotlight for designin clothes back then. And we didn't have no money to speak of to have her just makin shit up willy nilly. Momma Gloria usually made her own clothes, and a lot of mine, too, whether she was pissed at me or not.

She would draw out what she wanted to make like she could see it hangin in her mind, and put it down on paper. I used to sit and watch her sometimes when she couldn't see me spyin on her and just be amazed at how her brain just put stuff down. She'd take some money Herbert gave her and buy some second hand fabrics or scraps or whatever, or get somethin from a neighbor they ain't want no more and turn that into a dress or some pants or a fuckin scarf, you name it. I draw – got stuff all around my cell and in other spots all around this prison. I take my talent for that from Momma Gloria. But she never saw it. Never once did I show her what I could do. Bitch could flip on a dime and it won't like she was gonna say nothin positive about it, anyway, so I just hid everything I did.

Shaniqua found an old picture of Momma Gloria and was wantin to use it to draw a dress or somethin off of it. She showed me and said she was gonna make a dress just like the one the lady in the picture had on. I knew two things was true right then and there. Shaniqua couldn't draw a damn circle without a can, so she wasn't fittin to make no damn dress drawin. And I knew that the woman in the picture had to be Momma Gloria. The strange thing about the woman in the picture was that she was smilin just as high and wide as you please. And smilin wasn't some shit the Momma Gloria I knew ever fuckin did.

I saw the picture and thought go on, girl. So that's what you looked like before you started twistin your face and growlin at a bitch. Serves your ass right what you turned into.

I asked Herbert about the picture one day when Momma Gloria dipped out to go to Wayne's for some groceries. He took the picture and stared at it for a hot minute before askin me where I got it from. I pointed at Shaniqua, all bug-eyed like she was about to get beat, and he said fine. He started lookin at it again like it had been a long time since he saw it, or maybe that it had been a long time since he saw the woman in the picture. He didn't say a thing for a long time. And then he quietly just asked us to put it back where we found it. That was it. I wished I knew what was goin through his mind when he looked at the picture. I wish he would have told us somethin. Crazy thing is, I think maybe he said more by not sayin nothin than he would have if he had yelled or cursed and told us their life story. He ain't say a thing. But he said a lot.

☠♏☒♦

Of both Momma Gloria's babies even though I was the first – and I guess the source of all her misery – I have to think she tried her best by us. If I don't think like that, and I think about what I put my own babies through, kinda make me no better than her. And that's the last damn thing I want on my brain before I die. She raised us how she knew, and Latta wasn't no good example, either. I shake my head sometimes and think maybe she didn't have no business having kids. Paula didn't have no chance. She wasn't but two months old when she died. Herbert was crushed and Momma Gloria just turned more evil. I know now it was depression, but when you're little and your daddy's cryin and your momma's yellin and beatin you when she's not locked in her room cryin, and when you don't have no idea what depression is, that's scary and hard to deal with. Come to think of it, that's probably around the time I started actin out, acting tough and bein mean like her and Herbert. Not all the time, but when shit wasn't going my way, it wasn't nothin for me to turn it on. Sister tried to make me see that, but I didn't want to listen to her then. But the shit makes sense now.

And don't get me wrong. Sometimes I joke and say I ruined my momma's life, and sometimes she said the same. Most of the time she meant that shit. But the kicker is that she kept me. Never tried to get rid of me once and that tells me somethin. I wasn't a gift by any means, but I wasn't no piece of trash to just throw out. Momma Gloria saw somethin in me. Maybe like Sister does now.

If you think about it, Momma Gloria had every right to never have me. I've heard this story from her and from Herbert, and unlike other stories, they never change the way they tell this one. She was leaving work one night in New York City and got attacked. They beat the ever lovin shit out of her, took her bag, the little money she had in it from cashin her check, and raped her right there in the back alley of the cleaners like some dog. She said she could see people walkin by, not lookin her way even though she was screamin her narrow ass off for help. Everybody just kept on walkin. They ain't want to get involved. A short, thin little black woman was gettin raped, and ain't nobody want to get mixed up in whatever was goin on. In a black goddam neighborhood in New York! They beat her so bad and raped her up so awful she almost died. She crawled to the street and about got run the hell over before somebody called the ambulance to come get her.

City hospital took her in, but it ain't like they wanted to. No ID, no money, the bitch was unconscious and couldn't have told you her name to save her life. They cleaned her up as best they could, smacked her around a little to wake her up, gave her some aspirin for the pain, and kicked her back onto the street.

First time I heard this story and really understood what had happened, I must have been about ten or eleven. I knew stuff. Right? I knew the world had changed some, that black folk had more rights than ever. I knew that women was still strugglin but that they had respect and was fightin for more. I wanted to know why nobody cared for my momma when she needed it. I was smellin myself somethin awful and asked about the rape kit and the cops and findin the sons of bitches who did this to her.

Puddin, she say, ain't nobody woulda spent no money on no rape kit for a black woman then. And what you think some cops was gonna do? Nothin. And so that was that.

It wasn't a month later she found out she was pregnant.

Momma Gloria was nineteen and a virgin who got raped over $53 and a purse. Her life was ruined that night. What a way to become a mother.

☠♏☒♦

Momma Gloria had a way with words. But they wasn't always the nicest. She was for sure a storyteller and a talker, and most of the time liked hearin her own voice, whether she was talkin or singin off key. Remember when I said it sound like she be havin a piece of candy in her mouth when she talked? That was from the nerve damage she got when they beat her. Cut somethin in her mouth and because it ain't got stitched up or healed right, it's like part of her mouth died and kinda drooped. Made her words sound funny, but she could still yell and curse your ass out, funny face or not.

Anyway, Momma Gloria took to tellin the story of my birth one time maybe to the widow Rodney from up the street. They had coffee on days when the widow was more sad than usual and Momma Gloria would sit her down for some coffee and a piece of cake. I was still little, but remember I must have been ten or eleven. I told Sister one time before that I ain't a fuckin Huxtable, but she never quite understood what that meant.

Now to hear Momma Gloria tell it to the widow Rodney, no woman has had as much pain birthin a child as she did that night. Clawed the walls and screamed bloody damn murder. Her momma, Latta, was the one who delivered me. She'd made Momma Gloria come back to North Carolina after she got attacked, and that was the last thing Momma Gloria wanted to do. But she ain't have no choice. And let me tell you what's the truth – you think Momma Gloria was a bitch on wheels, and you ain't heard nothin or seen nothin like Latta. She died not long after I was born, maybe a year or so. She had the cancer and Momma Gloria said it took her pretty fast. To this day, I'm sure both of them evil bitches would blame Latta dyin from the cancer on me bringin stress on them.

I understand Latta was a big girl, and she look it in the few pictures of her that exist, and I look just damn like her. A mirror image from the big titties to the big ass to the big hair to the big mouth and cut your balls off attitude! I'm glad I got somethin of hers even though I never knew her. Like me, too, Latta was a fighter. She had to be.

Anyway, Momma Gloria clawed the walls and bled all over everything. Latta said I told you gettin rid of this baby shoulda happened long before now. Momma Gloria could have closed her eyes and let Latta do whatever she wanted when she pulled me out. But she reached her arms out waitin for Latta to hand me to her. Momma Gloria cuddled me all nasty and bloody before Latta washed me off. She was too young to be a mother. She ain't have no husband. No job to speak of. No prospects and a hard scrabble road ahead of her. She cuddled me, named me after the nurse who cleaned her up after she got raped, and kissed me on the forehead. That was just about the last truly lovin thing my momma ever did for me.

When I was about twelve, Momma Gloria's stories started runnin together. When we played the talkin game, we started goin around in circles like Momma Gloria, pretendin we ain't have the first clue what we was talkin about. That's the year Momma Gloria hit me upside the head and gave me this scar. I don't know lookin back if she was more pissed off at us playin the game or that we was goin around in circles or that we was pretendin we couldn't talk right. Either way, I paid the price for it. But turns out that was the first time we saw a crack in Momma Gloria's armor. Somethin wasn't right but there wasn't nothin we could do. Her stories got strange to the point where they made no damn sense. At one point, I think she got so turned around and so embarrassed – Momma Gloria was prideful as all hell – she just stopped. Ain't nobody gonna be makin a fool outta me, she told Herbert. And she ain't tell a single story after that.

No part of me wants to say good things about Momma Gloria, none at all. But what them boys did to her in New York put her on a path to hell. The beatin they put on her was like a time bomb. That's what the doctor said after she passed. Her brain was damaged so bad the doctor said he never seen nothin like it. It explains a lot. But it don't justify the way she treated us.

Here I am, sittin on death row writin about my life and tellin stories about how the world and this woman did me wrong. Somewhere out there, and I don't have a damn idea where, my babies have moved on with they lives like I never even existed.

Two generations of damaged goods.

I guess the apple really don't fall far from the tree.

June 12 (22)

Dear Diary –

Today Sonya returned for another session. Never before had I witnessed her expression of curiosity like she was wearing when she stepped through the door, promptly saying hello and sitting down in the chair in front of my desk. I looked at the guard who had accompanied her to me, and he shrugged his shoulders as if to say, 'I don't know.'

There is a hierarchy to the danger a prisoner exhibits, a classification, if you will, on their expected and reasonably assumed propensity for violence. There are some ladies you don't dare turn your back on, or for that matter, unshackle; murderers, those who have repeatedly assaulted individuals both inside and outside these walls, and miscreants tied so closely to an untreatable mental illness as to use my desk as a barricade whether they are fully ensconced in restraints or not. And then there are ladies like Sonya, who are non-violent and simply got caught up with the wrong crowd or were in the wrong place at the wrong time. Victims of circumstance abound.

Closing the door behind him, as is typical with prisoners like Sonya who represent no physical danger (although standing facing us, ready at a moment's notice to come to my aid), the guard retreated and Sonya leaned in. "Tell me more about your boyfriend and why you no longer a nun," she began, spitting the words out quickly as though she were hungry both for the rest of my story and to further associate her past with mine, ready and willing to learn from my mistakes.

I sat back in my chair and looked at what remained of her lovely features, ravaged over time by the effects of serious drugs. "What is your mother's name?" I asked. The downturn of her mouth told me that talking about herself hadn't been on her mind.

"Why?"

"Because my mother's name was Judith," I answered. "And she was a magnificent woman, unique in a lot of ways. I loved her very, very much."

"My momma was a bitch named Chantel." Sonya crossed her arms in disgust. *Damn therapy*, she must have been thinking. "I don't want to talk about her."

"Chantel is a very pretty name. Is it a family name?"

"I don't fucking know," she said. I sat there, silently looking at her, waiting for a nicer answer. "No, it's not." Sonya has so much promise, but also so much anger. Even speaking about her mother fueled something inside her that challenged her spirit and her ability to remain calm. "Chantel ain't no family name."

"And what is your ethnicity?" I asked. I knew full well that Sonya was biracial, Mexican and African American.

She shrugged her shoulders. "I'm a half-breed. My daddy black and my momma Mexican."

"Before such a thing as political correctness existed, Cher recorded a song of the same name." That clearly fell on deaf ears, and before I was asked who in the world Cher was, I moved on. "And did Chantel, your Mexican mother, know that you were a heroin addict?"

Sonya looked away from my gaze, trying it seemed, to find anything but me on which to focus. I don't know if it was subconscious or just a tick, but she rubbed her left hand and her breathing became more stilted. I asked again, more forcefully. "Yeah, she knew."

"And she was the one who introduced you to it, to Brad." Sonya began to tear. "Right?"

"Yeah."

"Do you love your mother?"

"I mean, I guess I do. She's gone, been dead for three years or some shit like that. What the hell you asking me about all this shit for?" Sonya was becoming agitated. I waved off the guard who had moved his hand to the door knob. You could watch the emotion well up, bubbling its way to the surface, and I just waited. I waited not for an explosion of rage or vitriol but for the release of the truth, the pain. "She was my mother! And she did that shit to me. I was her little girl! My goddam mommy gonna do that to me? I don't know why she thought she was gonna shoot me up. She was high, rolling on that shit I guess, and I came in. I was 13 for Christ's sake. How you gonna shoot up a 13 year old little girl?" She was sobbing uncontrollably at the memory. I wasn't sure where that firery emotion was coming from, but the catharsis was good for her. Sonya needed that release. You can only stay pent up for so long before the eruption. And before me sat a trembling Vesuvius.

I walked around my desk, sitting on its edge, directly in front of Sonya. "Last week, you told me that I should fuck God, and I agreed with you. Today, I'm telling you to love your mother now as much as I loved my own mother. Yes, she has contributed mightily to your being here, your troubles in life, your struggles to evolve and grow and contribute positively to society." I took her left arm and lightly touched the crook in her elbow, running my hands across the scars left behind by the needles. And I took her hand, pushed up my sleeve and let her do the same to me. The guard, agitated at my breaking the rules opened the door, but I waved him off. I'd take the blame and the punishment for whatever happened. He closed the door, scowling, but closed it and waited.

I told Sonya that we are the products of women who made mistakes in their lives. We are also the products of a loving and merciful God. We are stronger than we know. We are women and Beyoncé says we rule the world. She chuckled at that, and probably a little more at the fact I even knew who Beyoncé is. Black, white, Mexican, whatever, we are women first and we are amazing. Do you think a man could ever push a baby out of his body? Sonya laughed and said hell no. You and I have something in common and it isn't our mothers and it isn't our sex. We have an addiction. It is strong and tempting and dangerous and oh so very unsightly at times. But we're winners and we're going to have control over our addiction for a long time to come. Think about what your mother did for you – not about how you ended up here. Because of your mother, you've found a strength and a courage that might not have existed otherwise. Think about how you're going to be a role model for your own children once you leave here. Think about how you're going to rule your own little part of the world. And sit in a happy place where you're loved and you love others fully and with all of your heart. That is not where you are now, but it can be, it will be.

I sat on the edge of my desk, and talked to Sonya about the things she loved about herself, those things that were unique to only her. She mentioned something about fellatio that I won't put in print, but suffice it to say, apparently she was renowned for that prior to her incarceration. Less unseemly, though, was her love of mathematics, her ability to quickly solve puzzles, and her love of dancing. We didn't speak again of her mother or mine, or of Brad.

Before we knew it, our time was up. Thirty minutes can so quickly brush by you, can it not? Sonya and I hugged – absolutely against prison policy – and she walked to the door. For the first time in the six months of thirty-minute weekly sessions, Sonya looked at me and said, "Thank you."

And I melted.

☠♏☒♦

I walk into the dayroom to meet with Sister and she just kinda lookin at me. But smiling. I don't like walkin in when she look like that. Ain't nothin but trouble behind that smile most times, even when she tryin to be helpful. She must have seen the look on my face because she was like what's wrong? Bitch, I'm gonna be dead in like two weeks. Just like that the smile was gone, but I felt like an asshole for doin that to her.

I apologized and she said okay, but I don't think she meant it. I sat down and she started.

She started tellin me she just had a conversation with somebody else about they mother. Sister knows I hate Momma Gloria and I hoped she wasn't fittin to ask me about her. And, boom. She do. Sister starts talkin about how mommas are gifts to they children, and how without mommas wouldn't be nothin in this world. I flat told her she didn't have no damn clue what she was talkin about. And that she ought to be thankin her God that she ain't never met Momma Gloria or had the bitch as a momma. And then she asked me to tell her why. And don't roll your eyes at me, Janine, she said. I shook my head and smiled. Most times over these I don't know how many years, Sister felt more like my momma than my momma. If that makes any sense to y'all.

I looked at Sister and told her that Momma Gloria wasn't nothin but a loud ass, mean ass, big ass, swingin on your ass, rude ass, uncarin ass, scrunched up old face ass, schemin ass, lyin ass, bitter ass old woman.

Sister asked me what Momma Gloria taught me about life and bein a woman and momma and I said she ain't do shit for me. She ain't teach me nothin. Never had two kind words to put together after my name or about anythin I did. Wasn't me she loved, it was Shaniqua. Wasn't me she did shit for, it was Shaniqua. Wasn't me she wanted, it was me she got, and she was plain on makin me pay for that from the time I could understand what she was sayin to me. So, wasn't nothin she taught me I told Sister. And then the bitch flipped the script on me.

Okay, she says. Tell me about your childhood. Tell me what your mother taught you. Again, I rolled my eyes and she told me not to. Wasn't nothin to say.

Herbert worked a lot, off and on two and three shifts a day sometimes when he had to, when times was tough. He brought in money, loved me and Shaniqua the same, and sneaked us little stuff when he could. He didn't have no big education, but he helped with homework up until he couldn't and felt kind of stupid for not knowin more. He took us places when the car worked, and he went to things we had at school when he got the time off, or when he wasn't workin. And he kept me safe from Momma Gloria when he could, or maybe just when he was in the mood to fight her back. He got angrier and angrier as I got older and they used to fight more and more. I don't know why, but that's how it was.

Momma Gloria never did none of that for me. She dote on Shaniqua, helpin her with shit she never did for me. The golden child ain't know how to iron or cook or clean or comb her own hair or whatever by the time she was my age when I was doing all of that. A little girl, startin at six, maybe, and I got chores she never ever came close to thinkin about. Momma Gloria didn't seem to want nothin to do with me in public or in private. I damn near ran away when I was thirteen. The only thing I wanted was to be gone, to be away, leaving her and everybody else. After school one day, I got a bag packed with underwear and a dress and my dolly and some hair grease (don't ask me why I thought I would be greasin my own hair when I ran away! Haha), I stole some bread from the cupboard, walked right by Momma Gloria who just watched me leave, and I sat on the curb. I ain't have the first clue on how to really run away, clearly.

Herbert came home from work and parked the car. By now it was dark, maybe 7:00 or 7:30 and it was gettin cold outside. He had had a hard day, I remember him tellin me and wanted to know why it was I had sat my ass on the curb with a bag. You plannin on runnin, he asked. Yep, I say.

By this time, Sister just looking at me while I tell the story. Sometime you start talkin and it looks like you tellin her more than she thought you would. Like she's trapped in your head while you tellin the story and can see exactly what the hell you see, maybe before the words come out.

So I'm on the curb with Herbert. Momma Gloria and Shaniqua was inside, probably lookin out at me and him. He tells me to scoot over and sits down next to me. From the time I was born, he starts talkin, somethin been off about Momma Gloria. He loves her, he swear he does, but somethin about me made her the woman she is today.

Momma Gloria back then was a short woman, kinda plump and tired all the time after havin me and givin up on her old life. Herbert told me when I was littler than I was at twelve or thirteen that sometime Momma Gloria would look at me and start cryin. Ain't because she thought I was ugly, or because I was less than, but because I started off just like her. She knew she was treatin me just the same way Latta did her when she was a little girl. And it scared her more than she knew. And then she got madder and madder for some reason until when I was about two she just about gave up and she almost stopped takin care of me the way she should. That's when Herbert came back into her life. She was a rape victim, raisin a bastard baby, livin with her momma in a liquor house.

Don't get me wrong. Herbert wasn't no saint, and it wasn't like he ain't have no idea about Momma Gloria's past or what he'd be gettin himself into by takin up with her. I'm pretty sure he had a motive, too. Like I told y'all before Herbert was tall and skinny and redbone. But I think he might have been a little slow with the romance and not so good with keepin the ladies. I think he was married real young, but it went to hell and he ain't really get over that until Momma Gloria came back to Charlotte. He knew Momma Gloria when they was younger, before she set off for New York. He probably had a hard-on for her when they was little, but didn't know how to tell her. And then she was gone. When she came back, ten years older than her or not, he hopped on that midnight train like a Pipp, child or not, raped or not. They was two damaged people who found each other, and probably at the right time for me.

Sister asked me why I didn't run away that night. I told her I didn't know. She wanted to know if I thought it was Herbert who talked me out of it. I don't recall as to him ever sayin anythin tellin me not to run. He just talked to me. After a while, we just got up and went inside. Momma Gloria told me to put her goddam bread back and go to my room. Shaniqua just looked at me funny, like I was a fool or somethin. Herbert patted me on the head and whispered in my ear. I don't remember exactly what he said but I think I smiled.

And then Sister asked me about Shaniqua. I laughed and told her she'd be hard pressed to could cook her way out of a bucket. She certainly didn't have no idea about how to clean a toilet or mop a floor. Sister got me laughin about those times and how I used to hate that damn golden child. Shaniqua ain't somebody I talk to now – and haven't for the last thirty plus years, I guess. Like I said before, I love her cause she's my sister, and I'm probably supposed to still love her after everything. But we don't talk. She high style now, famous and shit. I don't talk about her and she sure as hell don't say shit to nobody about me. I do it outta respect for my little sister. I ain't tryin to blow up her fancy world. Ain't nobody's business she got a sister on death row. And ain't nobody's business in this motherfucker that I got a sister richer than all these bitches combined. We stay out of the other one's life. I can see her in the papers and shit, but it don't work the same for her. She don't even know what I look like now. But whatever.

.

So….Sister said. Like I was supposed to magically catch on. I'm just lookin back at her. Tell me what your mother taught you. Nothin. Must not have been listenin to my fuckin story, Sister. She still lookin at me. What is your favorite thing to do, she asked me. I answered without even thinkin, really. Cook. I love to cook. Or at least I used to. Kinda hard burnin when you locked up, I told her.

And what else? What else did your mother teach you?

Fuck me squared, Sister! Why we doin this shit? Why we even talkin about that nasty bitch? She ain't teach me nothin. I brought myself up. I learned to cook on my own, I learned to keep a house and a man on my own. I learned to put money away for the shit I wanted without havin to ask no man for money. I learned to keep my kids healthy and in daycare, and learnin and taught them that education – even a little bit of it - was the way out of any bad shit they gonna find themselves in. I had my own business and bought my house and a car and tried to do right when I wanted to and wrong when I ain't want to be right. I am a strong black woman who don't hit her kids or step out on her husband when I had one. I'ma push back when I have to, I'ma cut your ass when you don't pay me no mind and think I'm less than, and I'ma blast you if you even think about tryin me. Momma Gloria ain't have shit on shit on shit to do with none of that!

Sister didn't say nothin. She just smiled kinda small and let it sink in.

Until I heard myself.

Until I got it.

The Middle

June 13 (21)

I sat in the dark last night for a long time. Just thinkin about my kids. I mean, they was on my mind and I was also thinkin about shit that hasn't crossed my mind in a long time. My time walkin this earth, as little of it as I've got left, is almost up. That's some shit that hurts. I don't know why, but I think maybe I was takin for granted that I got one more day, and another and another. I ain't seen my kids in I don't know how long. It ain't funny, but it's like you lose track of time until you don't have none left. When I got that letter, my head was crazy and I was thinkin about everything and everybody. And then I wasn't thinkin about anythin. I'm numb. Right now I'm just numb.

If this book ever really does get made, I want to say somethin to all you women who got kids or maybe want kids, or maybe your babies got killed or locked up and you takin care of your grandbabies. Whatever is goin on, stop. Stop and hug them or kiss them or do they hair. Make them breakfast for dinner or lay in the bed and watch a movie or TV with them. Touch them and smell them and listen to the way they breathe and laugh. Don't just look at them and take pictures. Might be one day all you got is a picture and that ain't never enough for a momma. It ain't right to just look at the children you birthed and wonder what they lives are like now. I can't touch my kids. Even if they came to see me, which they ain't and which they can't, I can't touch them.

I can't kiss my girls or smell their perfume. I can't grab my grandbabies - if I even have any - and give them no sugar. I can't change no diapers or put on band aids, I can't grease scalps or brush hair. I can't listen to them complain about ordinary shit or scary shit or shit that don't make no sense. I can't wipe no tears or say things to them that's gonna comfort them. I can't feel nobody's arms around me that love me. Can't nobody pull me close ever again and thank me for somethin I did like makin Thanksgivin. Can't nobody squeeze me until I can't breathe and start laughin when I pop they behind. Out of sight, out of mind ain't never hurt this bad.

I sat here in my cell yesterday for a long time after my session with Sister when she made me think about Momma Gloria. I hate when she tricks my ass like that. Momma Gloria won't never be anythin more to me when I remember her than she was when she was livin and always treatin me like nothin. And I don't give nothin to her credit for the way she raised me. Don't no child deserve what came to me, and not the way it did.

I take all the blame for abandonin my kids. That shit was my fault and I can't take it back. But now I sit up in this cell, this goddam dingy ass tiny little cell, waitin to die. And they don't know that. I listen to my piano music and cry at night. They don't know nothin about what I'm goin through. And they don't care. I birthed them, brought them into this world, as awful and shitty and wonderful and scary as it's been for me, and for as long as I could, I did my best by them, and they don't damn care. And unless they tell me, I'll never know one way or the other.

That ain't somethin a momma should ever have to go through. No matter what.

☠♏☒♦

Dear Diary –

I wept today. I have wept most days lately. Not in support of one of my girls, and not because I was frightened by their limited futures and prospects should they escape this place. No, I wept today and before because I am still in love. And after this many years, going so long without temptation of the flesh, absolving myself of the need for his comfort, his passionate embrace, his knowing every inch of me inside and out, I am losing my fortitude, slipping closer and closer to that love which I had pushed deep inside. I am afraid I will succumb to the feeling and never be able to remove myself from its grip. That is why I weep. Because I am afraid.

I wish so many things for myself and others. I wish every day that my girls find comfort in the Lord, their Savior, Christ Risen from his tomb. I wish because I've stopped praying for them. I know how that sounds, Diary. It sounds as though I've given up on the faith which has been my crutch and my redeemer. It sounds as though I've dissolved the greatest relationship in my life. But you're wrong. I stopped praying for them because I've taught them only they can pray for themselves. I'm not the person to speak with God for them. That relationship, that commitment, is theirs and theirs alone to cultivate. It was a lesson I learned too late. That tiny seed planted in my psyche one day by Father Tervis, a seed I ignored and deemed unworthy of growing, has now blossomed and flowered into a truth I cannot escape.

And it breaks my heart.

In Peter I read, "Be shepherds of God's flock that is under your care, serving as overseers – not because you must, but because you are willing, as God wants you to be; not greedy for money, but eager to serve; not lording it over those entrusted to you, but being examples to the flock." My love, I fear, will make it impossible for me to shepherd, to prayerfully guide and teach these women in my care. His word, His grace, His wisdom have bolstered me for so long. I wonder why now, at this very moment in His timetable, does He no longer protect me from the love of my life? Have I forsaken Him? Does He no longer love and protect me?

Father Tervis told me God touches each soul independently. He knows when and where and why they need Him. But He hasn't seen that I need Him. Not yet. He hasn't seen my love coming for me, stronger and more resolute every day. He surely must know I'm in love. He surely must know I am not strong enough to defend myself against the advances. But He does nothing. I wish for the girls, I pray for myself.

Has He removed Himself from being my protector, content that I am no longer worthy? Does Psalm 34:19 not say, "Many are the afflictions of the righteous, but the Lord delivers him out of them all?" Nahum 1:7

tells me that "the Lord is good, a stronghold in the day of trouble; and He knows those who trust in Him."

And with each day that passes into the next, I remember the warmth of love into my core, falling more deeply in love. And, like today, I weep.

Brad loves me. And I fear he shall soon have me.

☠♏☒♦

The first time I got sent to jail – not my first time in prison…that's gonna come one right after the other – but the first time I went to jail was when I was a little girl, a teenager. That's when I told you about jumpin Herbert when he tried to beat down Momma Gloria after she caught him puttin his big old thing in Mrs. Sanderson. There was times when some really bad shit happened to me in jail. If I thought it would do any damn good, I might just set here and cry about it. The mean bitches and the bitches who wanted what you got, even though it wasn't shit but what the state gave me to keep from stinkin and my teeth from fallin out. I almost cut a bitch who tried to steal my soap, but just when I was about to shank her, a big old paw came out of nowhere and grabbed me. Probably the best thing ever happened to me besides my kids. I'd have killed that girl. Don't ask me why I ain't get in serious trouble for it. Somebody was watchin over me that day. I felt like Sister was watchin me, but she wasn't.

Sister likes tellin the story about how she first saw me that day in court. But I don't have no mind about it. I can't remember it all, and that's fine. Out of the blue one day, I get a visitor. That ain't never happen to me. Momma Gloria was content to let my big ass rot up in that piece before she stepped one foot inside to see was I dead or alive. Herbert sent me a card for my birthday sayin he missed me and wished I was doing good. Ain't that some shit? The bitch I was defendin can't pick up a goddam pen or a pencil and say two words to me. But the motherfucker I was tryin to teach a lesson the one who singin like a canary. Hell, maybe I should have jacked up Momma Gloria. Maybe that'd be a reason for her to check on me like Herbert. Shit makes me mad all over again just thinkin about it.

So, anyway, Sister was the visitor I had out of the blue that day. She was all smilin like some little puppy dog when I walked into the visitation room. I'm lookin around like who the hell came to see me? Sister called my name and the guard sat me down in front of her. I'm like, who the hell is you? Know what she said? I'm the only friend you got. Don't ask me why, but that shit made me smile, almost laughed a little bit. She had her nun outfit on and started talkin about Jesus and God, and how she was given the message that her life was supposed to be about helpin souls and some other crazy whack shit like that. I leaned down and looked under the table and sat back up. She ask me what I'm doin and I told her I was lookin for a burnin damn bush. When she was the one smilin, I knew we was gonna be alright, this strange little white lady, sittin in front of a little troubled black girl with ain't no family and no friends…until she showed up.

You know, I got a lot to say and not a whole lot of time left to say it in. I'm glad Sister came to the jail that day. I'm real glad she told me every damn time she could that I was a better person than I thought. I ain't much care for all of the religious bullshit and the way she kept tellin me that I was a child of God. But it was nice to have somebody to talk to, to tell somebody shit that I was thinkin and not get slapped for it, or made to feel like a piece of shit because I had an opinion.

Sister helped me understand a lot about myself when I was in jail, a lot of shit that I wouldn't never have ever come up with on my own. She came a lot while I was locked up, more than I thought she would. She helped me think about myself as a good person, but a bitch who got caught up on the wrong side of life at times. I'm not some genius, I ain't gonna ever make a million dollars, and it would have been a damn long shot for somebody like me to go to college and make somethin of myself. But from what I learned from Sister over all these so many fuckin years I been knowin her from the very start until today, I took a sliver of that white girl, busy body, nosy mother trucker told me, and made sure that I learned my kids better than I was taught. Sister did that for me, and I don't know if she knows it or not. Because of her, I was able to give my kids some real guidance, some real understandin of what it meant to live, to be black, and to be a woman in this world where there's times when nobody gonna give two shits and a nickel about you and your dreams. They was three and five the last time I saw them, the day I got hauled off never to see them again. But I know some way, some place deep in them, they know those first years of life under me was special. I have to believe that, even though I ain't heard a peep from them, I have to think that my lessons rubbed off on them, and they better people for what I been through, whether they witness it or not. I have to believe that.

See, turns out I wasn't supposed to be in jail or juvi or whatever it was for very long. The judge was tryin to make an example of me, make me think about shit I did wrong. And, honestly, I ain't really do nothin wrong except trust that Momma Gloria was gonna have my back when I had hers. But, whatever. Point bein, my time with Sister that first go round wasn't too long, maybe like four or five months. And would you believe she came to see me every week I was in? Blew me away. Hell, it still blows me away, if I'm tellin the truth. I got let out early, and moved back home. If you can believe that, right? I ain't have no place else to go. Well, long lived that wasn't.

I got busted on my second felony not long after getting home, two or three weeks clear, I think. I won't go into no damn detail, but just know that when you get hungry, and you need money to eat because Momma Gloria is treatin you like a slave and keepin food from you, sometimes you gotta rob and take shit from other people to stay alive. I never meant to hurt that little man at the Circle K. I needed money, he wasn't movin fast enough, and I punched him dead in his mouth. He fell to the ground and hit his head on the counter, knockin him the fuck out. I grabbed what I could, broke out, and hid from Momma Gloria and Herbert and the cops long as I could. I got spotted tryin to sneak into the park at night to sleep and got my ass hauled into jail again.

Turns out that the robbery and jackin the cashier and smashin him in the face and the brain damage he suffered all added up to a lot. I got put away, in a real prison, after just damn getting out not even a month before when I was 16 and ain't get out until I was 22. No Sister there for me that time. I liked to have died weeks into my first bid, but somethin told me stay strong. It was like Sister was there when she wasn't there like a goddam Jedi Mind Trick. Real early on, that bitch been in my head. Sometimes I liked it, and sometimes I didn't. But when she wasn't in my head tellin me to put down the knife or not to choke a bitch out or whatever it was I thought I had to do to keep my cred, and to keep from gettin jumped myself, it worked. Missed her so much, I even thought about lookin for her. But I didn't. Ain't have the first damn clue where to start no way.

That bid was worse than before. I had to grow up in prison, fightin what seemed like every damn day just to stay alive and keep from gettin it in the back. I counted down the days until I'd be walkin my black ass through them gates, and when I did, I turned around and gave that place the finger with both hands! For better or for damn worse, I was free – except that I still had to check in with my parole officer twice a week. I was ready to start my damn life over again, make up for some really bad shit I'd done before I got locked up, and also for some really, really bad shit I got away with behind bars. I couldn't go nowhere else, so yep, I went home again. This time was different. Herbert wrote me and asked me to come home when they released me. I thought maybe this would be the new fresh start I needed. The first two days out were two of the best and worst days of my life.

One more time, I ain't have no place to go when they let me out. I don't think he asked no permission before he sent me the letter, but Herbert asked me to come home when I got out. Not that he needed permission, I guess. But he said it in the letter. Over all that time, I never heard from and I never did see Momma Gloria once. You'd thought I was dead to her. And maybe that'd been better for everybody. Six years is a long time to be mad at somebody, especially when they can't argue back with you and give they side of the story, whether it's fair or you want to hear it or not. I sat up in my cell, readin the letters that Herbert sent me probably without Momma Gloria knowin. First, they was nice letters and he was tellin me about stuff he knew would make me happy, make my time go by. He sent me pictures and shit of Shaniqua growin up and turnin into a woman. He sent me jokes and shit and pictures of his work and of him fixin cars or whatever. At some point, he started talkin about Momma Gloria and how she wasn't doin too good.

Part of me felt great about that. And the other part of me heard Sister in my ear, sayin that whatever Momma Gloria was goin through was worse than what I got.

Remember early on when I said that sometimes Momma Gloria's stories would get to be where she said the same thing over and over again? Turned out she had a memory problem, maybe from that beatin she took long ago. Her brain fought it off for a long time until some of it just started to die and she couldn't remember stuff like she used to. And her stories would go in circles. Herbert said she got real bad and he couldn't no longer take care of her on his own. His body was battered after so many years of physical labor. His back and knees were failin him, and he told me that a doctor at the clinic found somethin in his lymph nodes, but Herbert didn't go into no detail about it. And remember that at the time he was only 52, 53. He relied a lot on Shaniqua to wash Momma Gloria and feed her and comb her hair. If I was 22, and Momma Gloria had me when she was near 20, she'd been 42 when she came down with that brain tumor, or maybe when they found what was probably there the whole time.

Now picture this: I get out of prison (they had me at Leath down in god forsaken Greenwood County, South Carolina). Leath was a L-3, and if you don't know shit else about prisons, know that you ain't got no candy stripers at L-3s. Bitches be scary at Leath and I damn near ran out of that place when I was paroled. Ran all the way back to Charlotte and I ain't look over my shoulder once. Only thing stopped me in my tracks was the site of my old house, where they were keepin Momma Gloria waitin on her to die.

By now, Shaniqua is a woman, seventeen. She know exactly what she want out of life, and she got a pretty damn good idea how she gonna get it. She ain't have to rely on nobody for her ticket out. Bitch was smart.

She used her goddam brain to get out. And the day I got home from Leath was the day she was movin out. My baby sister was goin to college. She waited for me to get home. I barely heard from her when I was down, but we was like them little girls in The Color Purple when we saw each other. Wasn't no African patty cake goin on, but we hugged and cried. You'd never thought we had a cross word to say about the other. In all the time I was down and she was stuck takin care of Momma Gloria, I can promise you she ain't call me outside of my name once. Not once. I just have that feelin. I just do.

I heard Momma Gloria screamin from her bedroom upstairs and I looked at Shaniqua like I got this. I got it now. I ain't been here for a long ass six years. You a woman now and you smart and you gonna make somethin of your life. I ain't about to throw no shade about you goin to college and forgettin where in the hell you came from. If I had the chance, I would have taken it in a hot second.

I kissed baby girl on the cheek and watched her walk to the cab, and roll away from me for the last time. I ain't seen her since. Not in person, at least. I see her in magazines and papers and I saw her on TV once for a hot minute.

I see her smilin and famous and rich as a motherfucker and free from her past. I see that little girl I used to protect and know that I ain't gotta beat up nobody. Because ain't nobody got anythin on my Shaniqua. She fierce. The hell with forehead, whatever her name is. She don't know fierce like my Shaniqua. I used to see her in magazines and for a long time, and even with all the other memories good and bad I have about baby girl and watchin her grow up, the only thing I could think about was how I left her alone with that monster. She was 11 when I got hauled off the second time. That's way too young for a girl to have to grow up. And in the short time Momma Gloria really started takin a turn for the worse, Shaniqua was forced to step up where Herbert either couldn't or just plain wouldn't. I was glad to see her leave, to spread her wings and get the fuck out of that situation. It was the last time I'd be able to really protect my little sister. I will always love her, but what kills me to this day even sayin bye to my sister for the last time is that it takes a backseat to Momma Gloria's infernal screamin the day I got home. For all baby girl's success I knew she was gonna find one day, the two things I still tingle over was watchin her ride away, and the way my neck gets tight to this day thinkin about that fuckin screamin.

June 14 (20)

This wasn't never supposed to come out. Herbert made me promise in the last letter he ever wrote me that I'd take it to my grave. But I can't. I have to break that promise I made. Might as well be in the grave now, I guess. And it ain't like Herbert gonna come back from the dead to fix my ass for tellin the secret. I just hope we don't meet up in hell.

I wasn't home two days when it happened. All night and all day, out of the goddam thin air, Momma Gloria would let out one of those screams. Sometimes it was low like a loud moan, and sometimes it was bloody goddam murder. Woman could wake the dead and she didn't even have to try no harder than she already was. And I get it. I get that the pain was crazy bad. Herbert was broke as hell, Momma ain't have a job in years, and neither of them had insurance you could hang a hat on. So the only thing left for her was to suffer all the way to the end.

You'd think I enjoyed hearin her, and I was sad for her at first. But then I got angry. Even when that bitch was dyin, she found a way to make everybody else's life a fuckin miserable experience. My first day back and she found a way to make me miserable from the jump.

I couldn't take it anymore that next mornin. I don't know why the neighbors hadn't called the cops on us. The sun wasn't even damn good and up and she just wailin. Ain't no way nobody wasn't hearin that. I had my face buried in a pillow, coverin my ears, but it didn't do no good. Momma Gloria was drivin me crazy and I just snapped. That's all I can say. I snapped, I lost it, whatever. I busted in her room and let her have it. I told her everything I was thinkin. She was half sleep on some old pain killers Herbert bought off the street if only to give himself a little peace and quiet a couple hours at a time. I told her she wasn't shit. I told her that the screamin and the pain and the torture was comin back on her ten-fold, a hundred-fold for the way she done me. Wasn't no God goin to comfort her. The devil was all up inside her, eatin her from the inside like she deserved. Momma Gloria was cryin mostly because of the pain, I suspect, but also because she was so mad at me for cursin her out.

Don't you talk to me like that, Puddin, she say, squintin through the pain. I'm yo momma and I deserve respect. You ain't been no kind of momma to me, I yelled. She tried sittin up in her bed and reached out like she was fittin to grab me. Get over here Puddin. You useless piece of trash. I'm your momma and you need to learn a lesson. I slapped her hand away and thought about spittin in her face. Herbert sat in a chair in the corner and didn't say shit to either of us. He just had his head down and was cryin. You a forty-two year old woman and you dyin. That shit ain't normal and it's what you get. Don't start none, won't be none. Remember that?

I pushed her back down on the bed, straddled over her, and I grabbed her hand and rubbed it on my scar on my face. Momma Gloria tried to kick me in my lady parts, but I was sittin on her legs, my full weight pushin down on her. She had lost a bunch of weight because she didn't have no real appetite and spent a lot of the day in bed, moanin and screamin. She tried to ball up her hand and I slapped her across the mouth. I feel ashamed of it now, beatin down a woman in her kind of shape. But I was achin with a pain not unlike what was torturin her, only my pain was visible and was comin through me like lightenin.

I told her it was long past time she was dead and out of my life. I told her Shaniqua left her ass high and dry because she couldn't take it no more. Momma Gloria saved me from Latta, but she spent every fuckin goddam wakin hour of every fuckin goddam day makin me pay for it. I was a baby, I was yellin. I ain't have no business bein treated like that. I grabbed her hand and rubbed it harder across my scar. You did this to me, you bitch. You the one ruined my life. You the one let them take me to jail when I was protectin you. Ain't never even bothered to come see me the first time I was away. And in the six years after that when I got put up for just tryin to find a way to live and eat, you can't bother to send me a letter or call my ass?

I remember Herbert just rockin away, cryin and cryin. I ripped into Momma Gloria somethin awful and would have kept on until she started coughin up a little bit of blood and her nose started bleedin real good. Herbert saw it and jumped up and got in between me and her on the bed. He grabbed me off her and pushed me out of the way and said that was enough. He wasn't yellin. He wasn't loud. He was as quiet as he was going to be. Momma Gloria and me was snotty and cryin and out of breath and he was strokin her hair gently. You could tell the pills was wearin off because she grabbed at her head and shut her eyes real tight a couple of times. She took Herbert's hand and squeezed as hard as she could, puttin some of the pain off onto him. And that's when I saw it. For the first time ever, I saw the connection they had. He loved her more than he could say. All the nastiness and the misery and the years of fightin and everything in between, they were meant to be together forever. She was in pain and his job was to take it from her, to make her feel better.

Herbert told me to clean up and meet him downstairs. He met me at the bottom of the steps and gave me two things: a safe deposit box key and $30. He told me to cool my heels for a couple of days and come back when I had some sense about me.

I went to Burger King and ate a biscuit watchin the sun get brighter and brighter and then I walked around until I got tired and slept in a park not too far from the house. I banged around for the rest of the day and slept in the park again that night. I went to the bank the next day to see what was in the safe deposit box. Herbert had stashed some cash in there even though he knew it was illegal. He also had more pictures than I ever thought existed. They were of me and Shaniqua and him and Momma Gloria. The deed to the house was in there, along with some other papers like the will and somethin about a family tree on his side. I didn't know what I was supposed to do with any of it, so I took some money and a couple of pictures, locked the rest of it back up, and dipped out of the bank. I laid out for a couple days like he said and went back wantin to ask him about all that stuff and where he got all that money from and why he wasn't usin it to make Momma Gloria's pain go away.

There was a little note in there and all it said was that he loved me and was gonna miss me and don't tell nobody about the note.

There was police and two fire trucks and an ambulance and a big black coroner van at the house when I got back. PoPo asked who I was and where I'd been for the last couple, three days. I told them I'd been doin what Herbert told me to and I was coolin my heels. I got sat down and that's when they told me. I thought it was strange that I couldn't hear no screamin. And where was Herbert? I was thinking that the whole time the cop was talkin to me and I had to make him say everything again.

Your parents are dead was somethin I ain't never thought I'd hear. Looks like a murder-suicide, but we're still puttin the pieces together. A neighbor called the police cause the screamin had stopped. Ain't that some shit? No screamin meant somethin was wrong. He said Momma Gloria got choked out or maybe suffocated with her pillow. There was some pills in the floor and some in the bed, and it didn't look like she struggled or put up no kind of fight, and they don't know if she took them or what or maybe she was unconscious when she was killed.

They found Herbert sitting up next to Momma Gloria on the bed. His brains were blowed out on the wall behind him. The gun had fell to the floor.

He was holdin her hand. Takin her pain and makin her feel better.

☠♏☒♦

Dear Diary –

I feel strange today. That's not right. I feel nauseated today. I read the North Carolina Department of Corrections Execution Protocol.

I should not have done that.

I know quite well Genesis 9:6. I understand that shedding a man's blood is a sin and that man, through His divinity, man is excused in shedding the blood of the sinner. But at what point does the circle begin and end? At what point is a murder for a murder not as barbaric as the act it was intended to punish, ne prevent? I am struggling today with my lessons for these women in my flock.

"For he is the minister of God to thee for good. But if thou do that which is evil, be afraid; for he beareth not the sword in vain: for he is the minister of God, a revenger to wrath upon him that doeth evil." That is Romans 13:4. I try and wrap my mind around that and then I read in Proverbs 9:10 that, "the fear of the Lord is the beginning of wisdom, and knowledge of the Holy One is understanding."

I love the Lord, with all my heart, and will for the rest of my time on Earth and with His grace, into an everlasting eternity. I sit in the stillness of the morning, or whenever I am most bothered by my hubris, to ask why man may kill man in the name and the image of my almighty God, but that to fear Him is the beginning of wisdom? At such an unseemly juxtaposition is where I've found uneasiness and the slow creeping invasiveness of cynicism.

The devotion to my Savior tells me that to question the word of my Holy Father is sinful and does so with a willful blindness to His plan and reasonings. The devotion to my flock, my sisters on Earth is also sinful and carries with it the same willful blindness. In my aching to be that to these women which they have been unable to find for themselves, and in my attempts at understanding the grace and omnipotence of my Creator, I more often have found myself running afoul with the direction I'm providing to them, and I feel I have begun to stray more from the path upon which I embarked sitting alone in that courtroom surrounded by strangers and sinners and the helpless.

Tonight, in this very small space of my consciousness, I feel as though I embody the pain of the unknown and dream of having my questions answered the day I stand before God in judgment, very deeply bent and asking for His forgiveness.

I think of these things as I read the Protocol. I wondered aloud if I should provide a copy of this to Janine, or even if I dare to mention it again. There must be solace in knowing how one will meet their demise. Right? Perhaps? Or perhaps not. Perhaps not knowing is the ultimate act of love God has for His children. We need not know His plan, but love Him until the day comes where it is put into motion.

I think of these things as I read the Protocol and think about Janine. From now until the hour of her death, I will harbor in my own thoughts the knowledge of each successive step, each rung up the ladder from which she will never descend. It is a powerful and tragic edification, especially since it cannot be shared. Janine is not the first person I've counseled as they sat on Death Row. She is the closest to me, though, and the shining light without which my own road to Elysium would never have been illuminated.

I read today how the last of her days would unfold and it made me sick. Unlike the general procedural understanding I had hoped to deliver that fateful day fewer than 30 days past, and the abbreviated countenance into which I stowed my emotion, today I saw that which I cannot unsee. I cannot look at her the same knowing that each time I do, I will have one fewer opportunity to repeat my gaze, to hear her laughter, to sense her trust and distrust; to feel her alive.

I think of these things as I read the Protocol.

June 15 (19)

The day I buried Momma Gloria and Herbert was back then, anyway, what I think was the loneliest day of my life. I'm just damn out of prison after a six-year bid. I hugged and kissed my little sister for the last time and watched her get drove away off to college. And the people I called my parents died together, on the same bed, on the same day, in the house where I grew up and returned to twice after bein released. No job, no money other than what Herbert squirreled away in that deposit box. For the first time in a long while, I was scared and ain't have a clue what to do next.

Didn't no investigation take place as to what was the cause of death. The police just grabbed up Momma Gloria and Herbert and took them wherever it was they take the dead before they get buried. Turns out funerals cost more than I ever thought. Dig a damn hole, put the casket in, and cover up the hole. Herbert, on the other hand, he'd been plannin this for while. I went back to the deposit box the next day and found the stuff he'd left there for me. Sneaky son of a bitch knew what was goin down, and he knew that layin it on me meant that it'd get done. The tiny ass little insurance policy he had on Momma Gloria took care of the simple casket and plot he'd bought. Wasn't no insurance on him, but he'd put enough in the box to make sure he got treated right, too. Nothin fancy. Just a couple of boxes, two of them no frills caskets, and two holes in the ground. His note said that whatever was left was mine for keepin.

I'ma always feel horrible about this, but without no way to find Shaniqua, wasn't no way she could even know they was gone, let alone find out about the arrangements. All I knew was that she was goin to college. I didn't never ask her where, and by the time I needed to know, the only people who could have told me was dead. We ain't spoke in years and years and years, but I know she holds that grudge against me just like I think I would her. And I don't blame her a bit. I might could have found her if I tried harder. But part of me just wasn't interested. It wasn't Shaniqua saddled with two dead parents. Wasn't her had to put them in they Sunday clothes and listen to the funeral man tell me how natural they looked. Ain't that some shit? Man fishin for compliments on the work he done to make Momma Gloria look like she still alive while she layin in the casket? I told him that if he wanted to impress me, he ought to try and put Herbert's goddam head back together. Yeah, he stopped talkin after that, little arrogant bastard.

So, even though Shaniqua wasn't a part of the plan Herbert hatched, I could have done better by her and tried to get word to her. She found out later that year when she wrote home and I was the one who wrote back, not Herbert, and told her. I can't imagine what that must have been like, readin some crazy unexpected shit like that. Know what I got back after that? A letter from my baby sister tellin me she was glad they was gone, and tellin me that now we were both free. I didn't know what in the hell we was supposed to be free from. Cleanin blood and brains and patchin a wall ain't what I call being free. Not havin no one to talk to about the storm in my brain and how scared I was at doin somethin stupid to get locked up again was crushin. Free from what? Fuck you, Shaniqua. She might have been free, but I sure wasn't.

There was two things I knew I needed to do. I had to get a job if I was gonna keep the lights and heat on in that house. And I needed to erase my sister from my life, just like she'd done all of us.

June 16 (18)

I did it again. Son of a bitch. I got sucked into this idea Sister got about me writin down my life story and usin it to teach somebody somethin. And I also looked up and saw the calendar this mornin. I feel like I'm wastin my time doin this. I don't know that nobody is gonna read what I write. And I sure as hell don't know that nobody is gonna learn a thing from my life. I'm so far from special, it's a joke. I ain't down on myself, and I don't think I'm any less than anybody else. But what is a woman sittin on Death Row, time runnin out faster than she wants, sittin here writin down anythin that comes to mind goin to do for anybody not in my same damn shoes?

I say nothin. And said as much to Sister. She just got that same old tired ass look on her face. And I just went right on back to writin.

Speaking of Sister, somethin's wrong with her. I can't put my finger on it, but somethin just ain't right with her. Been like that for comin up on a week or more. She's troubled by somethin, but hell if she's gonna tell me what it is. So I don't ask. I just look at her and wonder what's floatin around in that head. And look some more.

But I can't worry about that now. I got rememberin to do.

Yesterday I told y'all about how Shaniqua up and disappeared and I kinda let her. I needed to get me a job and I needed to find a way to stay in the house. Nothin worse than being a homeless ex-con. That combo don't go a long way in openin up doors, let me just put that out there. But before I roll down that path, I gotta back up just a little bit.

You might or might not guess by now that didn't a whole rub off on me in school. Like I told y'all before, Shaniqua caught up to me kinda fast, and then she passed me on account of me being in jail for so long. Math and me didn't get along. Grease and water. Pimp and no money. Snoop Dogg and no weed. Ha! That shit makes me laugh. Snoop Dogg and no weed.

Anyway, I didn't do school with any kind of success, whether it was math or english or geometry or you name it, the shit wasn't for me. And it wasn't no harder than anythin else I put my mind to, it just didn't capture me at all. Maybe if I thought about it hard enough, or tried more, school would have come to me like it did Shaniqua, but I was more thinkin about the rest of my life and how I was gonna survive. Plain that education ain't never got anybody out of my neighborhood, and only certain examples made a liar out of me. If Regina had kept her goddam mouth shut, she'd be out. And if I put my nose down in a book every once in a while, maybe I'd have got out, too. But gettin out because of your brain was hard to do. Not a whole lot of brain power goin into bein a garbage man or workin in the pipe plant uptown. So I didn't try. Right hand to God, I would have if I'd knew things would turn out for me like they did. Hell, maybe that's the lesson right there. Maybe that's the only thing Sister wants me to say. Read, bitches, and stay out of prison. You think? Ha! Snoop Dogg and no weed.

So, anyway, I got locked up when I was sixteen and got sent to Leath. If you don't know nothin about how they rank security at a prison in South Carolina, I wrote it down for you. You start at a L1-A. That's for bitches who got caught cheatin on they taxes or slapped a babysitter or some shit. It's low security. L1-B gets a little higher, and that's probably for bitches who threaten somebody or maybe beat down they man or a girlfriend. L2 is where the shit gets a little hectic because this is where medium-security starts. You got bitches here who think they run shit, but they just low level criminals who probably been runnin some drugs or somethin stupid. You got some dangerous bitches in L2, but not the serious kind – maybe they stabbed a ho at a club or accidentally killed somebody with they car. Okay, so last is a L3. That's where they put bitches with mental problems and bitches who kill people for the hell of it. This is serious lock down shit, high security, don't turn your back on a bitch in the shower kind of shit. You feel me? Now I'ma ask you why somebody who got busted stealing food to stay alive gets shipped out of state to Leath, a L3, with bitches who don't play.

You talk about the worst six years of my life, and it all started at Leath. Sixteen year old girl mixin it up with grown ass women. I was as scared shitless from the day I got processed into that motherfucker as the day I got processed out of that motherfucker. I saw bitches get shanked, I seen them lose teeth in fights, I seen them get knocked out so hard, they fell to the ground limp like a rag doll.

I kept my head down, didn't bother nobody, and did whatever in the hell I was told, be it by a guard or one of them bad bitches standin over me. Now don't get it twisted, I was still nice with my hands, and I'ma always be nice with my hands, but wasn't nobody in that place worth me gettin more than the six I already had strapped to my back.

I had a angel lookin out for me for the first five years and it wasn't Sister. Couldn't tell you where Sister was durin that time. Never showed up, never wrote my ass, nothin. But whatever, right? So this big old girl name Qu'enisha (honest to God) took me under her wing for whatever reason. I think she saw how scared shitless I was and didn't want nobody messin with me. Big Q – that's what we called her – didn't never ask me for anythin. Big Q looked out for me like I was her own. She never tried to get with me, she never made me do shit I didn't want to, she never raised her voice, nothin. She was like a big black 300 pound silver headed country Jedi because ain't nobody mess with her, and if they tried, somehow she just backed them down. Beat anythin I ever saw.

One day, about a year into my bid Big Q asked me what I was goin to do when I got let out. I told her I had no idea and she asked me about school. I told her I wasn't a good student and that me and class didn't really get along. I never graduated. I remember she laughed a little bit and smiled. We was sittin in the gym and some shit started to jump off. Big Q rolled down off the bleachers, walked over to the drama, squashed it, and walked off. When she came back, she had a book in her hand. I couldn't tell what it was from a distance and I hoped it wasn't no Bible or Kouran. She climbed her big ass back up next to me and put it on my lap. I don't want to see you back here, she says. Get yo' edge-cayshun. That's how she talked face all swoll and fat, pushin her mouth together on the outsides. Get yo' edge-cayshun. Don't bring yo' ass back hee-yuh. Dis what I use when I got my GED. I ain't nev-uh gettin out dis bitch, but you gots a cha-yunce. I got my GED cause ain't none these hos gone tell me they smart-uh than me. Best dayum thang I ev-uh did. You hear me?

I said I did and without knowin the why, I signed up for classes. It look a long four years and a lot of dodgin bitches who thought I was tryin to get over on them out of a book, but I did it. And it was the most proudest day of my life. They had a ceremony and everything. I laugh now when I think about all them hard bitches smilin as they walked in front of the class, wearin they silly lookin homemade graduation caps and gowns. These bitches would just as soon mean mug you for lookin at them the wrong way, but was smilin from ear to ear just from holdin a piece of paper. Half them bitches wasn't gonna see the light of day, but like Big Q said, before I had my kids, it was the best thing I ever did.

After the ceremony, I went to find Big Q. She got locked up when she was about the age I am now, so she was an old girl when she GOT to prison. I never asked her myself, but I heard tell that Big Q got locked up for killin this girl in a fight. Some say she was tryin to protect a friend or somebody she was kin to, I'm not sure. But she snapped. She went ape shit on her after the bitch hit her across the back with a pipe. Sixty years old and tough enough to take a pipe to the back and not get knocked down? What does that tell you about Big Q? For real, bitch was no joke. She got locked up for life after she chased her down (how you can't escape a fat bitch chasing you down, I'll never understand), jacked her ass up against a wall, and snapped her neck like a chicken bone. She ain't even fight when the police rolled up. Just laid on the ground, ready to take her punishment and get hauled off. I mean, what? Don't know if it's 100, but sounds like her from what I know. Don't nobody mess with Big Q.

Well, when I went to find Big Q, I followed the crowd into the gym. Wasn't unusual to have people fightin. Some shit flared up over some bullshit, bitches got loud, maybe somebody got punched, and the guards swoop in, case closed. Remember, Big Q's pushin 65 or 66 and she ain't have no business jumpin in. She was always the one to calm bitches down.

I came around the corner, right before the guards dropped in to separate bitches and saw Big Q lyin on the ground, in a pool of blood, bitches droppin shanks and scatterin like the wind. I dropped to my knees, not believin what I'm seein. Big Q was like a momma to me. I never told her. And I wish every day since then that I had. I made a promise to her right then. Nobody did a thing to help her. I got up and tried to break through the crowd, but got stuffed in the gut by a guard, knockin me down. If she wasn't dead on the ground, she was gonna be before they got her help. I promised her that I wouldn't take what she told me and showed me and taught me for granted. What I had in my hand, my GED certificate, wasn't a thought I had before her. Big Q showed me what it was like to be loved and thought of and pushed the right way. If I ever had any children of my own, Big Q was gonna be pushin them to, whether they knew it or not.

That last year was hard without Big Q watchin over me. I damn near sprinted out the gate when I got processed and released! Little did I know what the hell was gonna happen when I got back home. If I thought for a second I was runnin back to dead parents, I'd of high-tailed any place else.

You think about the people in your life that come and go when you lookin at what little time you got left. At least I do. That's what kind of shit crossed my mind lately. I think about the people I was good to and the people I was mean to. I think about all the things I wished I would have said to people like Shaniqua and told them how much I love them. All that shit is in the wind now because either they dead, they out of my life, or they don't know that I'ma be dead when they watchin the fireworks explode over they picnics and parties and celebrations. Independence Day takes on a whole new meanin when that's your last day on Earth. I don't give a damn about Momma Gloria, but maybe I'ma get to see Big Q when it's all said and done. Wouldn't that be nice?

June 17 (17)

Dear Diary –

I was taken aback this morning as I listened to the radio. They were playing *Somewhere Over the Rainbow*. I couldn't make out the singer, a young woman it sounded like, and one with a gorgeous voice. That song and its lovely melody and wishful attitude made me think about my mother. I asked Sonya the other day to tell me about her mother and listened to what she said, all the while thinking about the woman who did her best to raise me and my brothers.

That isn't a slight against my father, for he played a large role in my upbringing and the way I looked at the world. It is his devotion to Christ, in fact, that served as my example and lit the fire inside me when I was in my late teens, after my latest stint in rehab, and decided to become a nun and serve the Lord.

But my mother, oh she was something special. I wish I could have shared as much with Sonya but it would have been inappropriate. I'm not here to take these women down memory lane. I exist to help them come to grips with their lives and conditions as best I can; my mother isn't a tool in my arsenal, an arrow I can pull from my quiver in hopes they'll relate to my privilege and failure and resurrection. No, my mother and my reminiscing about her serves only me. She was the archetype of the kind of woman I despised internally but never let it show externally. Subservient, ingratiating, flawless on the outside with her soul all but hemorrhaging within, my mother was very disturbed. I'm sure, Diary, it is strange for me to say that my mother was something special, and in almost the same breath lay bare her mental illness.

I used to wonder what attracted one spouse to another. I listen to these women who come to me once a week and relay their life's experiences and what landed them behind the bars of a correctional facility. So often, their stories parallel that of my own, minus the extravagance I wallowed in. Mothers trying to keep the family together in the eyes of her peers and neighbors, whilst burning to relive the days of carefree womanhood, regretting her choices and feeling as though she succumbed to the inevitable. Husbands and fathers, and remarkably very few fathers in the home, working to provide for his family no matter the cost to the familial relationship. Why, one wonders, is it ingrained in men to work to a level of success attained because the values of family and love and God are the ultimate, if only silent, victims? 1 Samuel 18:14 tells us, "And David had success in all his undertakings, for the Lord was with him."

My mother is the embodiment of the pain and regret I see in faces and hear in voices from my flock. Day in and day out. My mother was special, yes. My mother was very disturbed, that is also very true. As the oldest child, and more so than my young brothers, I believe I more fully understood the anguish I witnessed raging within her; she was blissfully unaware of that, I believe to this day. I asked Janine to write, to teach, to inspire others, and it is something I wish my mother had not only said to me, but had done by example. "Listen, my son, to your father's instruction and do not forsake your mother's teaching." (Proverbs 1:8) I know she loved me and my brothers as best she could, leaving the discipline to our father, but she unknowingly left a void between us which should have been filled with love and kisses and the daring of each of us to dream big, to live a life much larger than her and much more fulfilling on every imaginable scale. Today, we simply call the anguish and emotion and imbalance boiling over in my mother schizophrenia. It was far more complex and frightening for a young family then, as I imagine it still is today. But we love unconditionally. That is what we did. It is what I wished for my mother.

Perhaps it was that void I was filling with Brad. It is a void I still yearn to have filled. Brad tried so hard the day he went too far. Brad tried to replace what my mother couldn't be for me, what I couldn't ask of my father, what was impossible for my brothers to provide. Behind the church that fateful day, alone with only Brad, crying and slowly succumbing to whatever it was I saw in me which I also saw in my mother. The reflection of her features, the less-worldly and impatient tone of her voice, the blind and fractured sense of duty to a man. The separation from reality and the breaks from sanity, no matter how brief. I shared that with her intimately more than she would ever know.

The memories I have of that day are scorched into the fabric of my being. I will never escape them. I remember the voices of the boys taunting one another, playfully pitting each one against the other to take me more aggressively than the last. I remember the way the cold felt on my bottom and my legs and the acrid smell of their breath and how Brad wouldn't let me move my arms or legs or scream or cry, pinning me to the ground, emotionless. I remember my parish priest, Father Tervis, praying over me. I remember my mother hovering over me in an ambulance. I remember her singing *Somewhere Over the Rainbow* through tears and the constant yelling of the paramedic. I remember crying because I didn't want to be her.

Today, I remembered how terribly I hate that song. And how terribly I miss my mother, flawed as she may have been.

☠♏☒♦

Okay, so I needed a way to make some money. What Herbert left me wasn't gonna do much about gettin me through the rest of my life. I went uptown in Charlotte to some restaurants and tried to get a job doin anythin. I'd have been a hostess or a waitress or dishwasher, it didn't make no never mind to me. I just needed money. I'd be fillin out applications, one after another, and every time, I got at stuck at that one damn question. Have you ever been convicted of a crime? Shit. I mark down yes and nobody gonna call me back. This application gonna go right in the goddam trash. I put down no, and when they check my history, I'd be just as screwed. I went to a fancy steak place and filled in everything but that question. Eagle-eyed little bitch at the front stopped me at the door, askin me all loud and shit in front of people if I'd been convicted of a crime. She said I must have missed that part. I looked her ass up and down, shook my head and walked out. Bitch knew that was gonna happen and just wanted to make a fool out of me. That's the kind of shit I don't appreciate, and the kind of shit that makes it hard for somebody with a past to get ahead in life. Some things ain't never gonna change.

One thing y'all don't know about me because you can't see where I'm livin is that I don't play when it comes to keepin my stuff neat. No, ma'am. Homie don't play that and neither do I. I can't stand a mess, ain't no reason for anythin to ever be dusty, and just like that singin white bitch flyin through the air under an umbrella, everything has a place.

When Gonzales brought me them crayons and paper, I'd do my little thing and put everything back in its place. My bunk is always made and it's sharp as a tack. My house shoes is always lined up, and the only other shirts and pants I got is always neat and folded. Since you don't get no real cleanin supplies in here, I took some scrap socks and wet dust every other day. Once a week, when me and Carlette and Blanche get our little hour of exercise time, they come and bleach down whatever ain't got fabric on it. Most people don't take too well to that smell, all strong and what not and what all, but I love it. Makes me know shit is clean. And it makes me think about my time on the outside.

Okay, so I had to get a job. Damn, I keep gettin off subject. My bad.

I had to get a job, and wasn't nobody callin a sister back for an interview or to tell me to go to hell or nothin at all. I was walkin back up the hill to my house when I saw my homegirl Sabrina Dinkins drivin my direction. Me and Sabrina been knowin each other since we was little, I mean since we was both probably on Similac. That's how long we go back. Bitch ain't left the hood, but she was doin it and doin it right. She see me walkin and stopped. She was like, what's up, girl? And I was like, ain't shit up, girl. You good? Ha ha, we had a short hand that I still remember to this day. She was like, girl I'm runnin like a long-tailed cat, bouncing my big black booty from job to job. I was like, I know. I be seein you comin and goin and puttin it down like a pimp. Sabrina got this look on her face like she got the best idea in the world and said did I want a job. She could use the help and I sure as shit could use the work.

Sabrina owned her own company, Sure Clean, and she went around Charlotte cleanin up after people. She'd been doing it for a while I hear, and got real good at it. She couldn't keep good help, and because she had so much to do and nobody to help her, it was like the business wasn't growin. That's why she was still in the hood. When I started helpin her, it was like we was meant to be together. Things took off for Sure Clean and we both started makin some good money. Of course Sabrina got most of it because it was her business, but she treated a sister right and pretty soon I had more comin into my account than I had goin out. That ain't happened to me in a long time, if ever, and I was over the moon.

I don't know why, but about two years in, Sabrina was blowin up and Sure Clean was makin her enough money that she broke out of the hood. At the same time, it was like she started gettin kind of cool toward me. I was workin like a dog for her because I was the best girl she had. She still had a hard time keepin good people, and I was her best, and she expected me to train these bitches to do everything like I did. And let me tell you that was a goddam chore in and of itself. I been cleanin since I was six years old. I know my way around a sponge and Pine Sol like nobody's business. Do it right and you ain't gotta use no elbow grease. Do it right, and what's gonna take some new girl twenty-five minutes to do, Janine gonna get done in ten. You feel me? You see where I'm goin with this? Can't nobody tell me nothin about how to clean.

Well, Sabrina fell ill so I took over some of her houses while she was down. Of course, she got all the nice shit, down there in south Charlotte where they be hidin all of the money. Bunch of white folks and bougie blacks sittin on piles of cash. You ain't never seen houses like this in your life. They was like little museums. All that space for maybe three or four people – a daddy, a momma, and maybe a spoiled ass little kid or two. My mouth fell open when I turned into the neighborhood for the first time. What in the hell do these people do was all I could think?

Well, I got to work right away and worked my tail off. Cleanin one of those places was honestly like cleanin two houses, that's how big they were. And since Sabrina usually went each week to the same houses, that's what I did, too. Sabrina wasn't really gettin better too fast, so a month or so went by and I still had her houses. My work was being covered by one of the girls I trained, so at least I knew what was gettin done was gettin done to my standards.

One day, when I was just about finished with this big old place, the lady of the house, Mrs. Bennett, walked up to me and said did I have a moment. She walked away and I guess she expected me to follow her, so I did. She sat me down on the sofa in the family room – and that was somethin you just ain't never did. You tired, take a break on your feet. Don't never sit down on nobody furniture, especially if they was home. I laugh about it now because when I sat down, I wasn't thinkin about breakin the rules. I wasn't thinkin about what this lady was wantin to say to me. And I wasn't thinkin about the rest of the day I had in front of me and the other shit I had to do before I went home and got off my feet. The only thing I was thinkin about was how goddam nice that sofa felt under my ass! Ain't that some shit? I was thinkin this wasn't no regular sofa. Must have been stuffed with the feathers of a million golden gooses or some shit like that. I was rubbin the sofa and squirmed around a bit and hadn't heard Mrs. Bennett callin my name to get my attention. If I was a light-skinned bitch I know she'd seen me blushing!

Janine, she said to me. I trust Sabrina to be in my home without question. When she said you would be replacin her for a time while she recovered from whatever she came down with, I was skeptical. I don't use skeptical and didn't really know what it meant, but the way her face scrunched up meant it probably wasn't good. So after the first time you came she said, I had you investigated. And that's when I started lookin around to figure out where the door was. And I understand you're an ex-con she said. You went to prison for stealing. Oh shit, here we go I thought. She fittin to try and blame me for some shit that came up missin. I'ma have to chill before I get black on this lady and lose my mind.

I have never she said had anybody clean my home the way you have. What? Did I hear that right? She kept on. You clean the way I would if

I had to do it myself. I don't know how I ever lived without you. Where the hell am I was what I was thinkin. And shiftin my weight a little bit more to feel that sofa. I don't want Sabrina to come back here. I want you to be my girl. I don't care about your record she said. All I care about is that you treat my home like yours. Like yours my ass, I said to myself. I could fit my house in this place over and over again. And before I knew it, she'd picked up the phone that was sittin next to her on the table I just dusted not ten minutes before. I ain't have the first clue who she was callin until she said no Sabrina Janine is to clean my home. She is marvelous and I simply can't function without her. That shit blew my mind. It blew Sabrina's too. I got fired the next day. Apparently, Sabrina felt better real soon. I was messin up her easy livin.

The joke was on her because I went back to Mrs. Bennett the day I got fired takin a big risk. I ain't even know if she was gonna be home, and I don't like bein in those neighborhoods without a real purpose. She opened the door, I told her I got fired from Sure Clean and she told me that was a problem. She had a scowl on her face. And then she smiled and said that she'd told her other friends in the neighborhood about me. And that if I was goin to be cleanin their houses, too, that I'd better come up with a name for my business pretty quick. Can you believe that? I was floored. In the space of two days, I'd got fired and formed my own business doin exactly the same thing I was doin before, but for Sabrina.

I took a chance goin back to Mrs. Bennett – God only knows what lies were told on me – and God only knows why she believed me and not my old boss. But she did. And that's how Janine Clean was born. I even had a little slogan. If it ain't Janine Clean, it just ain't clean.

That was a bright spot I hold on to real tight. I was in a great place and I thought life couldn't get much better.

June 18 (16)

You know how some people go to school to learn how to do certain things and be certain kinds of people. Like maybe some people go to school to be a doctor and some people go to school to learn how to build buildings and shit like that. And some people, probably like Shaniqua, go to school to learn how to work a business. Well, like I said before I didn't get along too good with school, and college was out of the question at the time. I didn't know how to run a business any more than I knew how to milk a cow. But just like milkin a cow, I figured it couldn't be that hard.

Now the first little bit I was up under Sabrina, I followed her around like a baby bird watchin everything she done. I watched the way she folded the clean sheets and towels. I watched the way she used one kind of cleaner on the toilets and another on the showers and sinks. I understood the timin she used when she vacuumed upstairs and then down, waitin until she ain't have zip left to do upstairs so she could preserve those neat little lines on the carpet, makin it look like maybe she'd made up the floor like she'd made up the bed. I watched it all, and took note of everything she was doin wrong.

Sabrina was heavy-handed when it came to things like pourin detergent in a bucket, and she ain't use enough water to cut down on how much detergent she was usin. That made it take longer to wash the detergent off the floor or whatever and not leave it sticky. And that meant she was usin too much water when she was rinsin everything down. It just goes in a circle.

See, I ain't tell Sabrina this even though she knew good and well I was down at Leath doin a bid, but when I was down I got put on the janitorial squad. You talk about cuttin corners and pinchin pennies, wait until the state gotta issue you some fake Pine Sol to use in cleanin the shower that three hundred nasty bitches stomp through every day. This gonna hit some of y'all the wrong way, but if you ain't never considered a bunch of bitches on lock down havin aunt flow about the same time every goddam month, you don't know shit about cleanin sheets and scrubbin toilets. Wasn't a job no man could do, let me tell you what.

At first, that job wasn't for me. Thanks to Momma Gloria, I'd already cleaned enough for five lifetimes. I may have been in prison, but I wasn't about to get stuck playin that Cinderella bitch again. And especially not for no bitches I didn't know and ones who'd just as soon shank my ass as try slip they tongue in my mouth. Hell no. I found out later that me bein on that crew was Big Q's idea and doin, anyway. One of the guards came round to the gym one day and called me over. I looked at Big Q like what did I do? I'm just sittin here doing nothin. The guard said I was now assigned to the janitor crew and that I'd better hop my happy ass on over there right away. I looked at Big Q and she just smilin. She said go on, child. We's gone talk bout it latuh. I wasn't happy at all about it, and I wasn't about to step on Big Q's toes and be ungrateful and look a gift horse in the mouth or whatever, so I went on.

This was about the same time I started those GED classes, yet another Big Q idea. I walked through the store room and into I guess what served as a big work room for the cleaners for the first time and I was amazed. It was like seein a bunch of elves workin on Christmas presents like when you're watchin commercials or Christmas specials. All I saw was girls movin here and there, some with buckets, some with mops and sponges, some with whatever it was they used to do the cleanin they were assigned.

The guard who walked me there nudged me over to a lady sittin behind a fenced window in a cage. I told her my name, she took my name badge and left. I stood there for a minute and she came back with some gloves and a smock. She handed me my badge and screamed over me for Stella. Me and the guard turned around to see this skinny flame-red haired old lady waivin me over. That's gotta be a wig was the first thing I thought of. Can't no old lady have hair that color, in prison, and be a hundred years old to boot. So me and my shadow walked across the room, dodgin the worker ants, and she introduced herself to me. Well, she kinda introduced herself. She said her name was Stella and that she'd run things for the last fifteen years. The other girl got shanked over some Clorox or some shit and they put her in charge. She handed me a key told me to check out the mop and bucket assigned to that key and to clean the floor in bathroom 3-H. And that was it. I looked at the guard and he smirked a little before nudgin me over to get my mop and bucket and cleaner.

3-H, I soon found out, was one of the dorms where they kept the old lady prisoners. It was for the bitches who got singled out by the guards as the weak ones, the bitches who couldn't handle where they were, and the ones who apparently had both poor bladder control and bad aim. The bathroom in 3-H was where they sent all of the new janitors and it was nasty as hell. You could smell it from outside the door. The janitors knew they'd be gettin a new girl so they let it get funky for a day, leavin all manner of nastiness in the bowls and on the floors. I kinda felt bad for the old bitches who had to put up with the stench, but then I remembered it was they old asses who created the problem in the first damn place.

Looked to me like the guard was about to turn on his heels and walk us back to Stella. He had a look on his face like he wasn't gonna stick around and watch me clean that place up. I told him if he wanted to go, that's fine. He knew where I'd be. And I got to work. Two hours later 3-H shined like a new penny. I think the chemicals burned a hole in my nose and I wouldn't get the image of poo out of my head for a day, but at least now all of them old bitches had a clean place to do whatever business they had to do.

I went back to the work room, checked my mop and bucket and cleaner back in, and gave the key back to Stella. She looked me up and down and smiled like she was some kind of gangster bitch or somethin. Good job, little girl, she said to me. What your momma call you when you were comin up? I should have lied but I told her Puddin. You like that name she asked me. Nope. Okay, then. I'll see you tomorrow bright and early. Puddin. I leaned my head to the side like I was about to say somethin to her and she raised her eyebrows. You did good today Puddin. You got somethin to say? I checked myself and shook my head. I dumped my gloves and my smock and another guard took me back to my cell.

I smiled when I thought about that, and followin Sabrina around watchin her waste money. She clearly ain't ever have nobody like Momma Gloria watchin her and seein how much of whatever she put in the bucket. And she ain't ever have nobody like Stella lookin over her shoulder makin sure that she could handle the nastiest of the nasty and keep her mouth shut. I was born and bred to clean and I knew it. Sister asked me one day what Momma Gloria ever taught me and maybe that was one thing.

And it served me good when I started my business. Sabrina's other girls always ran out of chemicals and sponges, and Sabrina always bitched and moaned about it, but she still gave them more of whatever it was they was usin too much of. And she wasn't one to do no complainin anyway, since she was doing the same. The way I figure it, all of them combined was costing Sabrina almost twice what it should have to keep a supply of chemicals and sponges on hand. And Sabrina from the hood, so she knows how to make a dollar out of fifteen cents (a dime and a nickel). Or at least I thought she did. No matter how we parted, I'ma say Sabrina always gonna be my girl for gettin me out of that tight spot. I appreciate that like hell and I hope she knows she saved a sister from doin some bad shit to survive.

Anyway, when Mrs. Bennett hired me after Sabrina fired me, it was on and poppin like fish grease. I started out on fire, cleanin her house from top to bottom, mindin my pours and mindin my supplies like I learned in Leath and like I learned bein up under Momma Gloria and like I learned watchin Sabrina throw money down the toilet. You ain't gotta pour half the bottle into the bucket for you to get things clean, and for it to smell like you did somethin. You ain't gotta use as much detergent as the box says to get sheets clean, either. And you ain't gotta spend all day goin back and forth upstairs and down, doin all the bathrooms and sheets in a group. I learned at Leath that timin was the most important. Bitches want they bathrooms clean, and the guards don't want to have to wait on no janitors to finish before lettin bitches take showers or dumps or whatever. Get in, be efficient, and get out. That's how I took to cleanin homes, too.

The second week I was cleanin for Mrs. Bennett, I hear somethin downstairs. It was Mrs. Bennett talkin to one of her girlfriends or neighbors or somethin. I was workin on changin the sheets on the boys beds and I hear the other lady askin if she felt like she was in danger for havin a criminal in her house, much less one that robbed and beat an old woman for money. I stopped in my tracks. Without a second of time, Mrs. Bennett took up for me. She said Janine was in prison yes. And yes she was there for stealin. But never did she beat anyone and she stole to survive, to eat when her mother wasn't providin. And you leave her unattended in your house the other lady asked. You have to give people a chance Mrs. Bennett said. I don't feel any more that she'll steal from me than she'd steal from you. Janine is a lovely woman who works hard and is damn good at what she does (she ain't say damn good, but you get the point). I was ballin I was so proud and happy hearin that and had to real quick wipe up my tears and get back to makin up the beds when I heard them comin up the stairs.

Mrs. Bennett could see I was cryin when she introduced her friend to me. I was surprised because the lady was black. She looked kind of rich like Mrs. Bennett, but I'd never seen her in the house or the neighborhood before. I looked back at Mrs. Bennett and I started to say thank you and she just hugged me. And that made me cry some more and I felt bad cryin in front of this lady I ain't never met before. Mrs. Bennett let me go and the other lady Mrs. Bednersh I think, smelled real deep and said what a fine job I was doin for Mrs. Bennett and did I want to come work for her once a week too. And I did for about two or three years before she died and her family sold the house and everything in it.

Anyway, I was workin my fingers to the bone, tryin to save every penny I could and tryin to figure out how I was gonna keep cleanin all these houses – I must have been up to six at that point – by myself. I didn't know a thing about payin taxes or whatever it took to have somebody under me, so I just kept on doin it all myself.

I was runnin a little ragged and gettin more worried about keepin up. But you know what? Damn if I didn't forget all about that – or at least put that shit on pause – the very next day.

All I'ma say is, "I loves Harpo. God knows I do." Hee hee. You gotta wait for the rest.

June 19 (15)

So I'm like 25 by now, I got my own business, I got my own money, and I'm doin good all on my own. I'm still livin in Herbert and Momma Gloria's old house, payin what's left of the mortgage after this long, and workin like a damn dog. After a long time livin where I came from, and goin through the crazy shit I did, it wasn't too often that I associated myself with white people. Sister was probably the first white chick I had any kind of friendship with, and that ended when I got out of jail the first time when we lost touch. White folks wasn't nobody we trusted when it came to doin a thing for us black folks. I look back on how they treated black folks for a long time and wasn't no real sense of warmth or hope I got from them. I can say today, right now even though I'm sittin in this cell, that that wasn't right.

What I mean is, and this is probably gonna sound real preachy to some people, and I guess that's fine. Most times, you hear what you want, anyway. But – and it ain't just because I'm gonna be put down in two weeks – you can't be puttin people in boxes when they ain't done anythin to you. I don't know if that makes sense. Like how Mrs. Bennett took up for me. No reason under the sun for her to do anythin like that for me. But she wasn't lookin at me as a bad person because I was black. I can't say she ain't look at me like I was less than because I was the one cleanin her toilets and washin her chidrens dirty clothes and sheets. But she took up for me based on just one thing: my ability. Wasn't a lot of white folks gonna to do that. And wasn't a lot of black folks willin to do the same thing if the tables was turned.

You gotta take the good with the bad, and you can't just assume somebody gonna be rude or mean or evil to you because they white – or because they ain't black. That was a hard lesson for me to learn, and it took a minute, even after Mrs. Bennett took up for me and spread my good name around her friends in south Charlotte. It was because of her that my business took off and that I was able to support myself on my own. Now, granted, don't get it twisted. Some of them white bitches thought they was gonna treat me like I was fixin them pancakes in the mornin and shuckin corn or pickin tobacco in the afternoon. They learned real quick that baby girl wasn't no slave and that I could up and leave at any point, leavin them high and dry. The worst, though, was the sisters with money who moved on up and wasn't fryin no fish in the kitchen or burnin no beans on the grill, if you know what I mean. It was my turn at bat and against Mrs. Bennett's advice, I gave a couple of them bitches down the road when they got a little too familiar and tried to speak to my just any kind of way, or try and get me to do stuff for free. Baby girl didn't do nothin for free. And you wasn't just gonna say what you wanted to me. They learned real quick. And the ones that didn't? Well, I'm guessin they picked up a broom or a mop until they found a simple girl to do they biddin.

I had just told off one of them, packed up my shit and drove to a Wal-Mart parkin lot to cool out. Back in the day, I'd have put my fist in a bitch's face, white or black, for tryin to tell me some shit like this lady had. But prison teaches you a thing or two and most of the time, although you see the same bitches in and out of facilities, most times you learn a good lesson: walk the fuck away. That lesson may keep you out a little longer than if you ain't learn the lesson, but still you learn that not all situations needs to be handled with your fists. Cussin somebody out and leavin them with they mouth hung open works just the same.

I was coolin off in the parkin lot when this boy walked by, pushin carts back to the store. He looked at me, and I looked back at him. First I was thinkin he was lookin at me because I was doing somethin wrong and I was gettin my speech ready. Ain't nothing wrong with sittin in a parking lot, so leave my ass alone. But he ain't approach me. He just kept on walkin and damn if he ain't smile at me. He up to somethin. That's what I thought. I just stared at him walk by, pushin them carts, and thinkin about cussin him out just like I just did old what's her name. He still smilin, he's still walkin. I'm still starin. He pushed those carts back to the store or wherever he was takin them and turned back around. I had a little more than a hour until I had to be at my next house. My own house was too far away, so I decided to run into the store and stock up on another bottle of Clorox and some sponges. Maybe piddle around and waste some time.

I walk in the store and this motherfucker is standin there just past the door, still smilin. I walk past him and go back to the cleanin stuff. I am mad and a little freaked out, but also a little horny for some reason. That shit didn't happen to me. I will say that by then I was thinner than I am now, but still curvy like a good woman should be. I wasn't squeezed into my clothes, and it wasn't like he could see anything from my neck down as he walked by my car outside. And then I thought about what I was sayin. Snap out of it, Janine! I laugh about it now. Why I thought that boy was lookin at me like I was doin somethin wrong outside, and then lookin at me like he had designs on me when I went inside. Ain't that some shit? The mind is powerful.

I find myself lookin at the Clorox and he shows up. I don't do a lot of mincin words, so when I saw him, in my aisle, fakin like he was straightenin somethin I walked right up to him. What the hell you doin followin me? You think I've done somethin wrong, you better come out and say it, or you better leave me the fuck alone. Boy, did his eyes get wide! For a second, I don't think he knew what to say. And then he looked at me and said I was smilin at you because I think you're pretty. I damn near dropped the Clorox and fell on the ground. And then it was my turn to not know what to say. I just stood there, like a fool, lookin at him. My mouth was hung open just like the old lady I'd just cursed out, but in a good way I think. I'd have swore that time stopped.

His name was Scot. I read that on his name tag. He had a cute smile, seemed like he had some muscle on him, he was taller than me. I really liked guys who were taller than me. And he was cute in the face. He said somethin about how he'd seen me in the store before but he ain't have the courage to say anythin to me. He saw me in the parkin lot and smiled. He didn't think I was comin in the store and thought maybe he'd smile. And then he saw me at the front of the store. And he didn't know why he followed me to the back of the store to the Clorox. And he didn't know why he pretended to fix somethin on the shelf that didn't need fixin. And he said I was really pretty. And he didn't know why he was still talkin. Me? I was still in shock. This boy was talkin to me. Like he liked me. I'd had my share of sex and boys when I was comin up, and a couple of fine ass men in the time I'd been out of Leath. But this was one hundred damn percent different. Never did I think I'd be so struck by the words. And never did I think I'd ever be hearin those things from a white boy.

June 20 (14)

I stopped last night after I started about Scot because instead of rememberin the good and fun and beautiful stuff, I started thinkin about the bad stuff and I couldn't put it out of my mind. And that wasn't how I wanted to tell y'all about Scot and the way my life changed when we was together.

I was talkin to Sister this mornin and told her that I wanted to tell about Scot, but that I didn't know how to start. She said that I should start at the best place I could. She said I should just start at the love. Sometime Sister comes at you from out of left field with some shit that makes so much sense you just shake your head. Start with the love. That's some brilliant shit. So I'ma start with the love.

After that day when Scot started talkin to me, my mind was blown. I actually remember not sayin a word to him, but smilin and takin my Clorox and sponges to the check out. I must have gone to my next appointment later that day, but I don't know. I couldn't think of nothin else but that cute white boy who told me I was pretty and how I wanted him to tell me that again. The next day, I went back to Wal-Mart to buy somethin I didn't need and looked everywhere I could for Scot but he wasn't there that day. I went back two or three days after that and didn't see him. I started to think it was a joke or a dream or somethin. Maybe I was crazy. And then I saw him again on a Saturday. He was at the Dairy Queen on Central, a long way from the Wal-Mart. I had stopped for a cone and I think he was as surprised to see me as I was when he turned around.

He told his friends two blacks guys and another white guy that he would see them later. They looked a little sideways at me but got in they car and disappeared. Scot bought me a cone and we sat on the hood of my car for I don't know how long. At first it didn't make sense to me, but most people like to have cleanin work done durin the week. I thought I would be busy seven days a week, and I was at first when I was tryin to get things off the ground. But when I could, when I had enough good clients, I was able to tell my weekend people that I was only open through the week days. Housewives want they weekends free to do whatever, and don't want to worry about nobody in the house when they aren't there. I got that. And I guess they husbands want they wives and kids available to do shit on the weekends they can't do durin the week. That meant I had a free schedule Saturday and Sunday. And that meant I could sit on my car and talk to Scot for as long as I could get him to sit with me.

Lord we talked for hours. The sun went down and we sat in my car. We made sure to buy a couple of burgers and some fries so we could stay at Dairy Queen and not have to go nowhere or get run off because we ain't buy anythin. I remember when I was at Leath Big Q taught me to say what was on my mind and that not doin that wasted more time than it earned. I started right off when Scot bought me that cone and I told him that I was 25, that I had my own cleanin business called Janine Clean, and that I had served time for stealin. I held my breath after I said the last part. He says to me. So your name's Janine? That's as pretty as you are. I pulled back my hair so he could see my scar. I'm puttin everything out there. To this day I don't know why. He took my hand and ran it along the back of his neck. That's a scar I got from getting hooked in a rope on my daddy's farm when I was twelve. I didn't know what it felt to love a white boy, but I was thinkin I could get used to how I was feelin right then.

He was 22 and was in Charlotte escapin the farm and small town life and small town minds. He worked at the Wal-Mart durin the day and waited tables at some fancy restaurant uptown at night. The guys he was with were waiters and cooks at the same place. We laughed about him bein a baby and he said I was robbin the cradle and I said how do you know I'm interested in robbin the cradle and how do you know I want to rob your cradle? Because you've been in the store the last three or four days when before that it was maybe every three or four days when I needed somethin. He looked at the smile on my face and told me I was even prettier when I was blushin. Honest to God I think I would have jumped his bones right then and there if my car hadn't been too small! That man knew all the right things to say. He asked me if he could kiss me and I said I wasn't that kind of girl. You and me both know I was lyin my black ass off. Haha. I told him I had to go on a date first. He asked me if I wanted to go on a date with him and I said yes. He asked if we could go to Dairy Queen. I smiled and said yes. And he asked if he could buy me a cone and a burger and some fries and sit in my car so he could tell me that I was pretty. And I said yes. And he asked me if he could kiss me. I laughed. And I said yes.

You ever seen white chocolate and dark chocolate melt together on TV or in a movie or just in your imagination? That's what it felt like to me. That's what it felt like when he kissed me. I wasn't thinkin about nobody watchin me or how nobody would react or how nobody had any business in my car or in my brain at that exact moment. He was kissin me and it was heavenly. He ain't try nothin forward. No tongue, it wasn't wet, nothin. I recall as I leaned in, I was lookin into his eyes right before we both closed our eyes, and I felt his hand come up on the back of my neck. That's when I felt him kiss me. And then I felt his hand touch my face ever so soft, kind of like he was cuppin my jaw or somethin. He pressed his lips onto mine and pushed ever so damn firm into me. I remember he smelled like cologne and hamburger. That was funny. I felt his hand rub the back of my neck under my hair (I had some good long hair then) and I felt his other hand or maybe his thumb rub across my cheek. I opened my mouth just bit and pulled his bottom lip into my mouth just a hair. And just like that it was over. He was leanin back and was slowly takin his hands off my neck and face. He asked if he could see me again, I gave him my phone number and he got out and disappeared into the night.

I had to get one more cone just to cool off, honey!

☠♏☒♦

Scot wasn't just my first love, he was my true love. Things wasn't always perfect for us. You can probably imagine what it was like a black girl and white boy in Charlotte comin up when we did, to have any kind of relationship. I started talkin earlier about not puttin people in boxes when they ain't done nothin to you. Well, I gotta tell you that the world outside the hood, and outside of the shit you go through in prison ain't always horrible. I found out when I was with Scot that there's this whole other world where white folks and black folks date and get married and have kids and live they lives just like anybody else, black or white or whatever. The hard part is on the other side of that world. The hard part of datin a white boy, and I guess it's the same for anybody who dates somebody not of their race, is the way people look at you and treat you and judge you and put you in one of them boxes I talked about even though they ain't got the first clue about you. I did that a lot to people, and it hurts to see what it's like on the other side of the words and stares and everything.

I took a lot of shit from white girls and black girls both for datin Scot. We'd walk through some place like the mall and it felt like I was gettin shanked left and right. They wasn't lookin at me like a criminal. The white girls looked at me like I was trash. The black girls looked at me like I was tryin to be somebody I wasn't. Bet if they knew where I came from, and that I was nice with my hands and that I invented curse words on the fly while I was puttin bitches down and standin over them, they'd have thought twice about mean muggin me the way they was. It was Scot, believe it or not, that made me chill. Ain't worth it, he said. Smile and keep it movin.

One time this bitch I clearly didn't know was gettin a little too familiar with me, thinkin she was gonna give me advice on life and stickin with my own kind. Scot squeezed my hand, stepped in between me and her yelled at her and told her to back the fuck up. He said if he'd wanted to meet and fall in love with a judgmental little jackboot faced troll, he'd have tracked her down. But as it stands, he was perfectly happy with the woman he'd already found and planned to spend the rest of his life makin love to and treatin like the queen she was. Left that bitch in her tracks as we turned and walked away.

I'm pretty sure that was the night our first child was conceived!

June 21 (13)

Dear Diary –

I woke up this morning and I was extremely happy. This is the first day since I learned of Janine's fate that I woke up after a good night's sleep, refreshed, and ready to take on the day. I looked through my bible for references of happiness and found in Psalms 37:4 the perfect way to express my emotion. It reads, "Delight thyself also in the Lord; and he shall give thee the desires of thine heart."

Oh how perfectly and wonderfully Psalm 37 spoke to me. It is with that enthusiasm for delighting in the Lord, my Savior, that I look to this day, this opportunity to bring into the lives of women and girls who come to me, the patience and understanding required for a life well-lived. I smiled – and, truth be told, I still smile – at the way my God entrusts me to be His voice after so many years having been abandoned by the Church. I thought back to Father Tervis but would not let his spirit or approach to his own flock leave me crestfallen in my zealous approach toward counseling my own.

I am happy that in this life well-lived, I have seen many splendid things, many miracles of nature and of God. I have met many unique souls, some of whom have been tragically damaged and left for dead. I have met many other souls who served as mentors and those who were resilient in their methods and taught me not only that God had a plan for me, but that His plan would be fulfilled whether or not I could call on the official recognition of the Church. They taught me that to be fulfilled by myself and my actions represented the first step in helping someone recognize that in themselves. I may walk with the Lord, but I lead those whose paths are lighted by me; entrusted to deliver those souls not necessarily to salvation for that is a journey one can only make for themselves, but entrusted to deliver them by word and deed from the evil that is their history, their environment, and their profound disbelief in what they are truly strong enough to accomplish.

I woke today, bright and full of wonder, full of promise to achieve.

☠♏☒♦

The oddest thing happened today when Sister walked into the visitation room. We both had this look on our faces, both of us smilin like that cat from Alice in Wonderland. She sat down and asked me first what I was smilin about and I asked her to tell me first. We both just looked at each other with these stupid grins. I asked Sister did she get some action in that old wrinkled puss last night and said no. Now she must have been in a good mood because normally, she'd have wrinkled up her face to match her puss, but said no and kept smilin.

I woke up this mornin, she told me, thinkin about how happy she was. It was right about then her face drooped a little and she realized she was talkin to somebody on death row. I reached out and took her hand, but the guard snapped and I let go. I told her it was just fine that she was happy. Can't pin your day and happiness based on what I'm facin. I leaned in and told her I was happy, too, even with somethin like twelve days left because I had the most amazin dream the night before. She asked me why and I told her because I had been writin about Scot before I went to bed. Sister knows everything about Scot, but sometime I think she tryin to live through me and asks me to tell her about him again. It's good for her and me to talk about him. A little more ain't never hurt, right? Well, here goes.

We went back and forth on this, him tryin to get me to agree and me all nervous and not sure, but after a little bit he won and we moved in together. We lived in little a house kinda out in the middle of nowhere, farmland, really. Back then Charlotte was growin but it wasn't nowhere near the hustle and bustle you read about today. Country and country life wasn't too far outside the city and city life, but it was far enough away from everybody that we felt safe enough livin as a white man and black woman. We wasn't married and it wasn't for Scot not askin me. He asked me plenty of times, but somethin in me said it wasn't somethin I was ready to do. I saw the love Herbert had for Momma Gloria, the way they hated each other at times and the way they used to abuse each other in their own way. That wasn't somethin I wanted for me and Scot. I ain't have the first clue why Herbert and Momma Gloria did each other like they did when they was livin, but if it happened at all because they was married, that wasn't gonna be in my future with Scot. Hell no. I loved this man. And he loved me.

I was real nervous at first, you know when we first got together and started datin because I wasn't sure why Scot was with me. I wasn't about to be no prize for a bet or some experiment. I laid down that law from the jump, after he kissed me that night at Dairy Queen, and I knew that I didn't want to be without that man ever again. I got scared enough to be real with Scot and he was real with me. He called me silly for thinkin what I was thinkin and he said I shouldn't be scared that he wanted me for any other reason than he just plain wanted me. I wasn't no trick or way to get back at his parents or give the world the finger. He saw me one day in Wal-Mart and knew that I was gonna be his. I told him I wasn't a project and that I didn't want nobody tryin to fix me or make me whatever it was they wanted. Scot put his finger up to my mouth to shush me. He said he wasn't lookin to change me, he didn't need to get back at his parents for anythin, and that he could give a fuck what the rest of the world thought or wanted.

I loved our little house. It wasn't much to speak of, really. A little brick house set well back from the road somewhere out where people think about Matthews, down 74. It was a cute little place. We could both get to work with no problem, we made a life together, and didn't nobody bother us. The night Penelope was conceived was magical, just the two of us in our perfect and special little home. Sister joked and said she wanted details and I told her she was nasty and wasn't gettin none of the good stuff from me. We laughed and laughed.

I don't know if it was just me, or if all women experience this, but that next mornin when me and Scot were just layin in bed, snuggled up and warm I just knew somethin was different. I can't say as I knew I was pregnant yet. I want to, but I can't. I just knew that my life was where it was supposed to be. I was born because my momma got raped and I only survived because my grandmomma ain't throw me in the trash or make Momma Gloria give me up. I grew up under the hand and thumb of a witch who treated me like a slave and didn't never say she loved me. I ruined my life early for her and she never said nothin to me in thanks. I went back to prison because she didn't have no cause to keep me and hold me like a momma should have. And when I got out, she died at the hands of the one person she never could be open and honest with, the one man who never left her side and in the end died next to her.

I woke up that mornin feelin different and special and right and excited and maybe a little bit horny, too. Sister got a kick out of that part. I felt the way his chest moved into and away from me when he breathed in and out and the way his hand twitched in mine because he must have been dreamin. I felt that little somethin on my rear that told me might be a little more this morning of what we had last night. But most of all I felt like maybe I did somethin right. For once in my life, I did somethin right. I let Scot into my life. I was honest and told him what scared me and he did the same. I felt safe. I never had felt safe before.

That's what I was dreamin about I told Sister. And that's why I woke up happy this morning.

Today gonna to be a good day for us both, she said.

June 22 (12)

It's possible that most of what I write from now until I write no more is gonna be about Scot more or less. Well, about Scot and the life we made and the babies we had. He was the love of my life and always will be. I'ma write about all that and about how everything can change on a damn dime if you're not watchin it.

That ain't a bad thing. The way I wrote that makes it sound like bad things happened when I got together with Scot, but that ain't true. I can't really think of nothin durin that period in my life that was bad. I had turned my life around, not that I was really a bad person from the start, just got handed a few bad cards. I didn't have Momma Gloria hangin over me. I was makin my own money. I had a beautiful man. And I was gonna have a baby. Scot got a promotion at Wal-Mart and he was now gonna be management material! Janine Clean expanded by two girls and I was gettin big as a house, just like Momma Gloria did when she was gonna have Shaniqua.

I'm gettin ahead of the story again. Let me see.

Scot was three years behind me, but you couldn't really tell that. He was strong-willed and pretty smart. Wasn't a whole lot he couldn't do or figure out a way to do. When we started datin, or I guess the kids called it talkin to back then, we had to keep us on the down low for a while. Wasn't a lot of black/white couples I knew of, and wasn't any that I knew of personally. Me and Scot were on our own little island.

I remember one day, we were sittin outside Eastland mall, I think, when this white girl walked up to us. Me and Scot both got a little tight thinkin we was about to get into an argument with this lady, walkin all fast and aimed right at us. She stuck out her hand and said her name was Barbara. Me and Scot looked at each other and then shook Barbara's hand. Without invitation, old girl sat down next to us on the bench and started askin us questions. How long you been together?

How did you meet? Does anybody give you a hard time about bein together?

Scot and I kept lookin at each other wonderin if this was some kind of joke or if we was gettin set up for somethin. I can usually smell the okie doke from a mile away, but that was different.

Seven months. At the Wal-Mart in south Charlotte. All the time, but we just deal with it.

It wasn't until we looked up and saw this black guy walkin toward us that Scot started figurin it out. Brother stuck his hand out to Scot and said his name was Bryon, and it looked like we'd already met his wife, Barbara. Ah ha. Another couple like us. I was a little stunned, if I'm tellin the truth. I ain't know what in the world Barbara was up to, and she just about got told off right before Bryon walked up. Me and Scot just laughed and laughed at that one. Bryon and Barbara was apparently new in town and when she saw us sitting on the bench, she made a B line right for us. We just moved here from Maryland and you're the first interracial couple we've seen she told us. I hope you don't mind us introducin ourselves.

I think it was at that exact moment that me and Scot kind of exhaled a little bit, breathin a little easier or somethin. We were alone. I mean, of course there were other couples like us out there, but until just then we didn't know any of them. The white guys were supposed to get with the black girls because of their big booties and sex drive. And the black girls…well it was rare, really, for black girls to date or marry white guys. I never figured that one out, really. The only ones that comes to mind are Iman and David Bowie. But he's weird, so I don't know how much that counts. But most of the time it was a Bryon and Barbara kind of deal. Black guys loved the white girls for whatever reason and even though black girls used to say white girls was stealin they men and black guys was abandonin they black culture, there's plenty of black girls who either got on a white boy or dreamed about it at one point. There just wasn't a lot of them who did anythin more than that.

We did everything together, us and Bryon and Barbara, because we was all about the same age. Bryon was a loan officer for a bank. I don't recall which one. And Barbara was a paralegal. I was fascinated by them because of how different they were from me and Scot. To me, we were simple people makin our way in the world. They were professionals. They had good jobs, made money, talked different than me and lived in what I used to call a white neighborhood. We lived a long way from each other, so when we got together it was usually in uptown Charlotte or a place we all decided on. Until I had Penelope, it wasn't often they came to our house on the other side of the city.

Right after I had Penelope, maybe a month or so, Barbara came by to see me and the baby. She took the day off work and brought us lunch and said we were just gonna stare at the baby all day. I had told Scot before she got there that day that I was nervous about her comin. He asked me why and I said that it was because I didn't measure up to her, and wasn't no way I ever would. No tellin what she really thought of me when not around each other. She's got fancy friends and works in an office and wears nice clothes to work with her attorney bosses. I clean houses for a livin and don't know my their from there from they're most of the time.

He was about ready to walk out the door. He set his lunch pail and coffee down and took my hand. I remember it was my left hand because I had Penelope in my right. He took my hand and we sat down on the sofa in the livin room. He told me I was bein silly and I told him I wasn't. He told me from the day we met Bryon and Barbara, he'd kept a hard line in his brain about makin sure not to get too close to them. Scot was good at pickin up on people and he could sniff a fake or a rude person out in a hot second. He used to make sure and stay reserved when he met new people in case they tried to hurt us or use us for some reason. He said he never got that feelin from Bryon or Barbara.

He said he never told me this but the day I had Penelope, and Bryon and Barbara were out in the hallway, he saw their true colors. Scot had peeked his head out to get their attention to come in, but saw Barbara givin our nurse down the road. She was pointin her finger in the nurse's face and you could tell Bryon was tryin to make sure to stay in between

Barbara and the nurse. Scot said he walked up to the group and the nurse, a white lady, and she turned four shades of pale. Hell, I don't even know if that's a thing, but it sounded good. She starts stammerin out an apology talkin about how she was sorry if she offended us and that all babies are beautiful and that she worked at that hospital for twenty years and hadn't seen a mother and father no matter their race who loved their baby more, and that she didn't see race, and that all babies was precious, and blah blah blah. Scot said thanks for the apology and looked at Bryon and Barbara and they just winked.

Come to find out, that nurse was standin at the nurse's station and was sayin somethin to the other nurse who had checked Penelope right when she was born, and she thought she was out of earshot of anybody who knew me. She said somethin Barbara didn't like and she shot out of her seat like her ass was on fire and got in that nurse's face. She was talkin about how she does legal work for the hospital and started throwin around names. The nurse ain't have no idea that the names Barbara was throwin around wasn't in no way connected to the hospital, but her face got all ashy and she got red too, and Bryon stepped in and that's when Scot walked up.

Scot rubbed my cheek and rubbed little Penelope's hand. He told me not to worry. He told me that Barbara would have my back, fake names and all, in anythin. Wasn't no judgment from her. He kissed me and left out.

When Barbara showed up about two hours later, I couldn't help myself. I broke down cryin and told her what I was feelin and what Scot had told me. And how I was sorry for feelin that way and that she was free to leave. She was standin at the front door. Know what she asked me? Was I just gonna stand there or was I goin to let her in? She told me all about what the nurse had said and said she was about a hair's thickness from punchin her in the mouth and fightin her before Bryon stepped in. She told me she loved me because she was my girlfriend and she would defend me and my baby from anybody who got in her way. Class and jobs and money didn't have nothin to do with how much or why you love somebody. You just do. Penelope started cryin, and then I started cryin more, and then Barbara started cryin right along with us. I think we were all maybe cryin for different reasons.

Penelope was wet. Barbara was feelin my pain. And I realized for the first time in my life, really deep down and genuine, that I had a girlfriend of my very own.

June 23 (11)

Penelope was born in October, so her first real Christmas wasn't until the next year when she knew more of what in the hell was goin on. You want to know the best feelin in the world? It's buyin presents for your baby and husband at Christmas. Scot and I exchanged a little somethin the year before, and the year before that, but money was tight between his Wal-Mart job not bringin in a whole lot and the expenses like Clorox and Comet cleanser even after his discount and gas for the car that went into Janine Clean. Over time things got a lot better, but in the beginnin we kept it on the cheap.

Scot started doin real good at his job and went from assistant manager to junior manager or somethin. Didn't make too much sense to me. I thought the assistant manager was the junior manager. But he came home all proud and I thought better about askin him questions about somethin silly like the difference between assistant and junior.

Well, Janine Clean was doing good too, and I had a little extra in my pocket to hire another couple girls because we had got up to about ten or eleven houses. And I'm talkin about monsters. One of them had to have two girls all day long because it was so damn big. That was fine with me because the bigger ones paid more money.

One thing you gotta realize is that even though we didn't have much money when I was comin up, we all found a way to make Christmas special some kind of way. Well, everybody but Momma Gloria. Buyin presents was pretty much not done, so we made stuff for each other. Wasn't nothin crazy, but it was the thought that counted. The first year I was able to buy Scot and Penelope real gifts, and more than one, is somethin special to me and somethin I never thought about havin the chance to do.

We sat Christmas mornin when Penelope was 15 months old and laughed as she tore through the wrappin on the way to a box with a doll or a soft little stuffed bunny in it. Once she got by the paper and saw what was in the box, she just moved on to the next thing. She could have cared less about the toy or the doll. She got so tired rippin through her ten or twelve presents that she wanted to eat and then take a nap. It wasn't until she woke up an hour or so later that it hit her…all those things were for her. And then the excitement started all over again.

I walked back into the kitchen after makin sure Penelope was playin okay and saw a hurt look on Scot's face. I'd got him a nicer watch for Christmas than he'd been wearin. I went into Charlotte and bought it at a real jewelry store. It wasn't somethin I got from Wal-Mart on special when he wasn't lookin. It was a gold Timex with a metal band and everything. I asked did he not like what I got him and he said he loved it and smiled. He put a piece of paper on the counter and slid it toward me. I shook my head and had him read it aloud. It came to him so he should read it.

When we got together some time back he was livin in this house. I was in Herbert and Momma Gloria's in west Charlotte and that worked for a while. Ain't nothin like tryin to sneak your white boyfriend into your house where nosy eyes couldn't see. And then tryin to sneak him back out. That was some mess I didn't want to hear from the people around me who ain't have zero business in my life or tellin me what about nothin. So when things got more serious and he asked me to move in with him, I jumped at the chance. It wasn't Regina gonna be my way out, but Scot. Well, durin the time he left his parent's home and came to Charlotte and met me, he was still writin his momma letters to tell her he was okay. He said one time he got a pretty bad letter from her and he wouldn't tell me what she said but that he wouldn't be writin her again.

Scot started readin the letter and I pretty quick knew it was from his momma. And she wasn't happy a bit. At first I was mad that he told her about Penelope and that our life together was wonderful. I ain't have the first clue why he stopped writin her, but when she said that I was a mongrel and he was raisin a mongrel baby, I saw why he probably stopped. Like a lot of folks, his momma and probably his daddy wasn't ready for a black anythin in the family. And I didn't place blame on them for that. I might should have but I didn't. Wasn't my place to judge how they felt or tell them how to feel. Everybody feels things different. Puttin right or wrong into things sometimes ain't your place. It doesn't do nothin to make it hurt less, but you sometimes gotta look at things from the other side.

I can't imagine a momma tellin her child that she never wanted to see him again unless he changed his ways. That meant leavin your baby and the baby's momma. He finished readin and brought Penelope back to the kitchen from the livin room where she was playing. Scot looked at her and then me and said this is all the family I'm ever gonna need.

That was far and away the best present I ever got.

June 24 (10)

Dear Diary –

I sit today and write having returned from a funeral. It was a simple service, as simple as a Catholic service can be, I suppose. Simply walking into the church took my breath away; as though God pulled my breath from my body only to replace it with His own, letting me know that it was still He to whom I prayed and for whom I kneeled down. St. Joseph was the closest to the prison, and with the considerable effort it took to get permission of the Monsignor, it was a lovely place to say good-bye to Sonya.

To see so much of oneself in the face and embodiment of another person can be both delightful and frightening. I saw my past in Sonya, her tender face slowly destroyed by the effects of a drug introduced to her by a mother either too young or too stupid or both to know better. I know what Brad can do and he's taken me down a path I wouldn't wish anyone travel. For reasons only known to God, I have been able to shy from Brad's full grip. And although there are certainly times when I can feel the rush of him and the ease of his touch coming over my body, it is with God's strength that I can resist. I absolutely can do all things through Christ who strengthens me.

In me, Sonya had an example of what is possible when one commits their life to one of betterment, of service, of sacrifice, and to the ultimate love of a father who gave not only His son, but His mercy and wisdom such that we could create a life for ourselves in His image of caring and protection. What delighted in me and frightened Sonya was, I feel, the idea of loss. She hadn't yet seen the wonders opened up to her once Brad was no longer part of her life. Living without him wasn't something she had prepared herself to do. Her mother had died of the same thing, a heroin overdose, leaving Sonya in the clutches of a boyfriend and family members less concerned with her well-being than her ability to contribute financially, to do her part. Pushing heroin made her money, and it kept a roof over her head, the ultimate consequence be damned.

There are those, I imagine, who would see this scene of mourning laid out before me, the urn and the solemnity of the few family members present, and should they have been privy to our conversation where she cursed God and I followed suit, be just in their assuming her death was vengeance. They will quote Nahum 1:2 wherein it is written, "The Lord is a jealous and avenging God; the Lord takes vengeance and is filled with wrath. The Lord takes vengeance on his foes and vents his wrath against his enemies." That is not true and I have no empathy for such a view. For the Lord is loving and *A Prayer for David* tells me so. (6:7) Give ear, O Lord, to my prayer; listen to my plea for grace. In the day of my trouble I call upon you, for you answer me." Sonya was crying to the Lord for help and he has brought her home, freeing her of pain and shame and guilt. She is among the angels now and it is we who are left on earth who struggle with her departure.

As I sat in the sanctuary and listened to the Holy Sacrifice of the Mass, I thought not of the myriad ways that poison was entering the prison and how to stop it, how to save another Sonya. No. I sat and I wondered if my own funeral will be so sparsely attended; mourners few and far between. Will Janine's?

I write today prior to my first session knowing full well that I will be comforting Sonya's friends with rote chapter and verse, reflexively almost, and helping them to understand the plan the Lord has written for us all. Some will accept what I have to say, and some will not, seeing through my memorized words and feeling my deep loss and embarrassment for failing to help such a fragile soul. What I hope they do not see is the envy I carry for the end of her struggle, her final and most desperate escape.

☠♏⌧♦

I have ten days left. I have ten days left to breath and feel and cry and smell and touch and taste and and and. And then nothin. I will be nothin. I won't be a wife. I won't be a mother. I won't be a friend or a lover or a enemy.

In ten days, I'm just gonna be nothin.

June 25 (9)

Hi. I think I want to apologize for yesterday. I had a real bad day yesterday. I couldn't write more than that. I started thinkin about a lot of shit and couldn't focus on what I wanted to say. I had to put everything down, put away all of the fuckin drama and just cry. Heck, girls do that. Even sixty year old bitches on death row. Right?

So I am sorry for not writin yesterday. I told that to Sister because she made us talk. She wouldn't cancel our meetin. I told her I had a lot of things in my brain that I wanted to get out, but it was like everything was fightin everything else. And the only thing that won was nothin. Just silence. Sister didn't try to talk me into nothin and didn't get rollin on no scripture. She just said she understood and we sat for a long time before she got up and left.

I got nine days left. And by now I'm bettin y'all are trying to figure out why the hell I'm in here. Why the hell I'm on death row. And if that's true, if none of y'all is from Charlotte and you just readin this out of the blue or for some legal class or because you sick enough to read the last writins of a dead woman, my story ain't no more different than anybody else in my same boat. Hell, there's two more bitches up here with me. I don't know what they done, but it must have been fucked up enough for a judge to tell them too that they gonna be put down. I don't know and I don't want no part in askin. That's they business, just like mine is mine.

Anyway, I think when I left y'all before, it was Christmas and Scot's momma sent him some nasty ass letter talkin about gettin rid of me and Penelope. He didn't take too well to that if you can imagine. He said he loved his momma so much and that wasn't anythin like this ever said or showed in his house when he was comin up. He kept tryin to tell me his momma wasn't no racist, but part of me thinks he was tryin tell himself that she was. And just like everything swirlin around in my head yesterday, his head was full of stuff he didn't know how to take or deal with so he shut down a little.

Wasn't like that for me because I always knew where Momma Gloria stood on everything. Wasn't no sugarcoatin nothin with her. She ain't like my hair. She ain't like my body shape or my clothes that she damn made. She ain't like my attitude. She ain't like white people for doing her Momma Latta like they did. She ain't like this and she ain't like that. I can't recall thinkin one time that I was ever close to Momma Gloria. Never. Dead and gone and I don't care because I'm free from her. Yeah, she haunt me every now and then, but nothin shocks about her or that. Scot is different because he sounded like he hung on his momma's every word.

I have to keep tellin myself that she wasn't no bad woman. Carrie was her name. She was just tryin to protect her baby, I guess. Can't say as I agree with the way she was doin it, but I can't a fault a momma for wantin the best for her kids. And on paper, that sure as shit wasn't me.

Bein so young when we got together, I sometimes worried about what kind of future I was gonna have with Scot. You know what I mean? Our lives were totally different from the jump and maybe it was that we wasn't supposed to even get together, but some how some way we did. I don't think Scot had a plan to leave his momma and daddy and come to the city – Jesus, don't that sound country as shit – and find a black girl to piss them off. I don't think that at all. We never really sat and talked about the real reason why he left, but from the way Scot talked about his parents, you could tell wasn't no negative reason. Been on this farm his whole life and wanted to know what else was out there. It's a simple enough dream, I guess. It makes sense to me.

Carrie and Victor – that was his daddy – must have thought maybe he'd come back to the farm and let him go to the city thinkin it wouldn't be long before he'd be back and doin whatever it is you do on a farm, milkin cows and cuttin grass or whatever. It ain't funny to some, but it sure as shit is to me thinkin about the way their face must have damn turned up when they read in a letter that he was dating a black girl and she just had his baby. I'ma bet you Carrie fell out. That shit is funny to me, even though it probably ain't to some. But just like mine, Carrie's world flipped on a dime from some shit she read in a letter. The count down to killin me and the way her family now included a black girl and a half black baby. Ain't that some shit?

Was supposed to be a day and time when anybody can marry anybody. Ha, for a long time me and Scot had pet names for each other. He called me Mildred and I called him Richard. We ain't do that outside the house because wasn't no point in gettin people confused. But at home and in private or whatever, or like when he engraved the bracelet he gave me when Rebecca was born and wrote Mildred on it, that's what we called each other. Might sound like not sexy or dumb names to you, but Mildred and Richard were the reason me and Scot could be together in the first place. It was the only court case I ever got familiar with, really, because it was a mirror of me and Scot. Loving against the state of Virginia. Me and Scot. Mildred and Richard. I guess Carrie didn't know nothin about that and maybe it wouldn't have mattered one bit to her, anyway. But me and Scot loved each other and that's all that mattered.

That Christmas when Scot said his family was the present he wanted, I read the whole letter from Carrie when Scot took Penelope after lunch to clean her up and then lay her down for some quiet time. Not even Momma Gloria could have said meaner things. I won't rewrite what she said. I still remember it. I can still see the hate on the page. I remember just standin there and cryin and readin and wonderin why I was still readin. My heart hurt knowin that this was the woman that birthed the love of my life. She was the only grandmother my child had left in this world. That letter sealed off any hope of my Penelope knowin that hateful woman.

And to think that she could say all of those hateful things and not even know me was what took me aback. I mean, everybody is gonna say somethin about somebody they don't know. That's plain and it happens. But it's one thing to talk about a bitch or somebody around the way you've seen before or maybe know somethin about because somebody else said somethin. But to call somebody dirty and a criminal and no good? Aw, shit. Said I wasn't gonna rewrite what she said. Dammit. Point bein Carrie didn't know nothin about me or how I took care of her son or how I worked my ass off after comin up from nothin. If anythin, and fuck me for sayin it, I was a model goddam citizen. Who else you know went from convict to successful business owner and mother and long term girlfriend smooth as I did? I should have been gettin a medal instead of some far away bitch trying to cut into my life and break up somethin she ain't never even witnessed.

Lord, now Carrie got my pressure up.

Scot and I didn't keep no secrets between us. We both agreed when we first got together that secrets didn't do nobody any good and probably did more to hurt the other person than just being truthful. He walked back in the kitchen all quiet like he was sneakin back after puttin Penelope down and swooped me up into his arms. Scot was still real fit and handsome all through my pregnancy and as I started to get the weight off – well, the weight that would come off, that is – and he always told me how much he loved holdin onto me real tight like he never wanted to let go. He was feelin a little horned up if you know what I mean and went in to kiss me and I moved my face. That's when he saw I was cryin and when I told him I read the letter and the things his momma had said.

Damn that man. He pulled me closer to him so much that I could smell the aftershave left on him from the day before and my face tickled a little from his rough face on my cheek and ear. Ain't never gonna be without you Mildred. Come hell or high water or my momma, ain't never gonna be without you.

I wish that had been true. I wish to Sister's God and your God and anybody else's God that that had been true. Age don't have anythin to do with it, I guess. Yeah, Scot was young when he left for the city. But more than anythin what got him, what took him from me came down to the way he loved his momma.

☠♏☒♦

Dear Diary –

I had a most wonderful surprise today. Jonathan Stouter, Janine's attorney, paid me a visit today. I ran to the door when I saw him and hugged him and hugged him and hugged him. I told him, perhaps more forthright than I should have, that I hadn't expected to see him again; that the young attorneys rarely, if ever, witness the execution.

I should have measured my words and waited for him to tell me exactly why it was he'd come to me today, because the look on his face told me that I'd overreached, that he wasn't going to witness the execution, that I was correct, and that he was now extremely embarrassed because I'd put him on the spot.

Thankfully, he took the high ground we both took our seats in the arm chairs in front of my desk, and he rolled right on with the conversation. "I've come by to let you know I have implemented a letter writing campaign for Janine. I'm trying to get the governor to issue a stay of execution." My heart sang, perhaps even literally, and I hugged him again. He continued and told me that since it had been several weeks without a response from anyone, he wanted to tell me in person that things weren't going to the way he'd hoped. Letters were being written by a cross-section of the Charlotte community and were mailed to the governor, both senators from North Carolina, state representatives and anyone else who might have a single shred of influence with the Office of the Governor. I asked how many letters had been sent and his sheepish reply said enough. It was hard to find more than thirty people to write letters on her behalf was what he all but whispered.

"Her crime was such that…," he started before I cut him off. He was clearly in pain, suffocating from the helplessness choking him. It blocked reason and hope, simultaneously, leaving very little room for optimism. I agreed that her crime was likely holding back supporters of a stay. He touched my hand softly with his and quietly, almost uncomfortably, asked me if we could pray. And so we did.

June 26 (8)

I saw Chocolate yesterday! Damn he's fine. Young, but fine.

You don't get visitors on death row. Nobody but your lawyer and somebody like a spiritual advisor or counselor can see you. Normally, the only other person I get to talk to is Sister. I say a couple things every now and then to the guards, especially Gonzales, but by and large I keep to myself. Been keepin to myself for so long, I don't really know how to talk to nobody but myself and Sister. But I had to talk to Chocolate so I paid attention and tried to concentrate on what he was sayin to me.

I'ma be honest and say that I was lookin more at his cheek bones than listenin to him. But I keyed in on the part when he said people writin letters about me to get the governor not to kill me. That shocked me. I wonder did Penelope and Rebecca know about the letters and maybe Shaniqua. Well, not Shaniqua, but the girls. Did the girls know they could write a letter and more than that would they? Hell, could Chocolate even find them? It's so close now, doesn't seem like nothing can slow down this train.

Chocolate always gets this look on his face when he got somethin bad to tell me. I hope that boy don't play poker because somebody gonna take that pretty face for all he's worth! He looks at me and says he don't want to get my hopes up and that writin letters might not work. He kinda winced like I was gonna blow him out the frame or maybe give him down the road. I just shook my head and told him that none of this was his fault. He ain't put me here, and he ain't to think he's responsible for not gettin me out of here. Swear I almost saw him cry. And, Lord, watchin Chocolate cry is the last thing I wanted to see. Ha!

I asked him if Sister wrote a letter for me and he said he was gonna see her in a little bit and that he'd tell her, and that he was sure she would. I told him the bitch better write me a letter and he froze. Jesus, I hope Chocolate loosens up a bit real soon. That motherfucker gonna have a heart attack if he don't learn to chill and laugh at shit every now and then.

I told him what Sister was makin me do, write down everything I wanted to tell about my life. I told him that Sister said somethin about turnin it into somethin to help young girls and women walk a path different than me. Chocolate smiled and said that was a great idea. He said that he would do what he could to see that it got published. I nearly fell out when he said that. I ain't never really considered this to be somethin that would get seen by anybody but me and Sister. But to hear Chocolate say he thinks he can do somethin to get it published blew my mind.

It made me think about how I said stuff in the beginnin and that I maybe want to change some things. I was real pissed and short in the beginnin. But then I changed my mind. I'ma be me. Somebody said that but I don't know who. And I agree. Besides, I couldn't change nothing anyhow because Sister got most of the pages and she ain't fittin to give them back so I can clean up some cussin or spell some shit right. I'ma be me.

Those was the only things Chocolate had to say, I guess. He got up, and when he was gone, Gonzales took me back to my cell.

Today is a new day, and one more gone. I don't know that Chocolate knows I know, and maybe he don't either, but this is my last day here. I mean my last day at the women's prison. Death row bitches get moved to Central Prison which ain't too far from the women's prison I'm at now to wait out the last week before they get killed. They call it Death Watch. Huh. Ain't that some crazy shit?

Remember when I snapped at Sister for tryin to tell me about what I was gonna expect now that shit got real and I had a date? And I told her off? Well, I went behind her and got all that information on my own. If anybody was gonna know what the fuck I'm lookin at, it's gonna be me and I'm gonna read it with my own goddam eyes and take it in without nobody sittin over me. And that's what I did. I ain't want no surprises and trust a sister when she tells you that she know everything that's gonna go down, right to the last damn poisonous drop.

Like I know tomorrow I gotta pack up all my shit and get carted through gen pop (general population for y'all) and paraded past some new bitches who probably only heard about me, but never saw my ass. I imagine some truths and lies been told about me, and since other than playing in the library on Tuesdays which I ain't done for a long time now, the death row bitches are kept apart from the bitches who got a chance to get out of this place on they own two feet, I'ma probably blow some minds tomorrow. And I love it. I'ma walk with my head up, strollin past them all. "Pretty women wonder where my secret lies. I'm not cute or built to suit a fashion model's size. But when I start to tell them, they think I'm tellin lies." That is still some of the best shit I ever heard. Thank you, Maya Angelou, girl!

The only thing I want to take is this picture on my wall of me and my girls. It was taken a couple of weeks before everything went down and it's what I held on to for all these years. I know that they ain't look nothin like they do in this picture. I remember buyin these little matchin pink sweaters for them and greasin scalps and puttin them in these little puffs with the balls on the end. Why I remember that day so clear and so much else up and vanished, I don't know. But I'm glad I held on to this in my brain. I know everything's changed for them and not only the way they look. Hell, they little girls here in this picture, and in the real world its some thirty odd years later. Girls grow up into young women and they grow up into wives and one day maybe grandmothers. I used to draw them with crayons and imagine what they look like as the years went by.

I had a lot of pictures, stacked up on my little writin desk. They all got ruined about ten years ago when the sprinklers went off because some dumb bitch started a fire in her cell. I was so down I just stopped. I didn't draw nothin else and thanked whoever is upstairs that no harm came to my one real picture. I might have had it on me or close to me and grabbed it real quick to save it, I don't recall. And so this picture is all I got of them. I told Gonzales to find a way to make sure this picture finds its way into my casket. We'll see if that happens. And except for my writin, they can burn all the rest of this shit in this cell. I got no use for none of it.

☠♏☒♦

Dear Diary –

Matthew 18:15 "Moreover if thy brother shall trespass against thee, go and tell him his fault between thee and him alone; if he shall hear thee, thou hast gained thy brother."

Luke 8:17 "For nothing is secret, that shall not be made manifest; neither [any thing] hid, that shall not be known and come abroad."

I need so desperately to speak with Janine, to impart upon her a secret I have kept from her for so long it almost seems fictional to me. A bend in time created a rift between us, and one that has never been addressed or filled. The time has certainly drawn nigh for such a conversation, an explanation, a pleading for forgiveness and understanding. The eve of her death draws closer, and with it the inevitability that she will go to God knowing the truth about me. I pray it is a conversation that will be gloriously painless for us both. And I pray for the wisdom to know how very wrong I am to think such a thing.

June 27 (7)

Moving day.

I have my picture. I couldn't carry nothin with me. Everythin was here when I got here.

I walked passed those gen pop bitches lookin straight ahead. Not because I was tryin to be strong. But because if I looked at any of them, I was gonna cry. And that shit was NOT happenin.

I hope I get to see Sister today. She's the last bit of normal I got left. God knows I need it now. This place ain't suited for nobody who ain't dyin, but it ain't right to leave somebody who's gonna die in a gray and lifeless place like this. It's more like torture than anythin else. Guess I'm the only one gonna get killed this week. I'm by myself up here. There ain't no leavin my cell for showers or to eat like I did in the other place. I got my things, but I got nobody to talk to. Shit, even when you're alone at night layin in your bed, you could maybe still talk to the guard who might be watchin over you. They was people too and we all need to talk to somebody else every now and then. If nothin else just to hear the sound of somebody's voice talkin to you in a way that meant they wanted to know what you was thinkin about. Gonzales was real good at that. He made you feel like you wasn't a piece of trash, that maybe you had a brain and some feelings and that maybe he wanted to know what you thought about stuff every now and then. They was alone too all night so it only made sense to talk. It ain't like that here. The guards don't know me. I'm just another number in the way of them gettin a paycheck, somebody they gotta escort down the hall in seven days and don't got to worry about seein anymore or ever dealin with. Just maybe ought to call this place dead end.

The Ending

June 28 (6)

I got word this mornin that Sister been tryin to get over her to see me, but the rules is tighter here and she had a little trouble gettin on the list. I don't know why since she's the only person I wrote down that I wanted to come see me. She's allowed and her note said she'd try and come tomorrow. It made me happy to know that. Seein her will help make this place not as scary.

I had a rough night last night. Bein here and away from everybody I was used to is like what I guess it feels like to be in solitary or shoved in a hole somewhere where there ain't nobody else to look at or talk to. This place even sounds different. I can't hear the TV that was down the hall and I can't hear any traffic because the window is to high and to thick for sound to get down to me. Shit, the light has a hard enough time comin all the way down here. The walls and the floor and the bed is all the same color. It's cold in here and the bed ain't for shit. But what do they care? You're not gonna be here no longer than a week. You can be comfortable when you're dead, right?

Sounds like I'm complainin about this. Maybe it is. But I know exactly why I'm here. And I'd do it again in a hot second.

Not too long after Penelope turned about two or three, I got pregnant with Rebecca. I had a pretty easy pregnancy just like I did with Penelope. I ain't want for nothin and Scot was being the same gentleman and nervous daddy he was when Penelope was growin in my belly. Everythin seemed the same, except it wasn't. Scot was really doin good at his job and it meant he was movin up in the company. Part of that movin up meant that he had to take on different shifts at different stores, some of them clear across Charlotte. It was great for us because he was makin really good money and we was able to save more than ever before. Janine Clean was doin good too and I had five girls working for me. I couldn't do a whole lot bein pregnant because of the chemicals and stuff so I mostly went around and checked on the girls. Some of my houses paid me in cash and didn't write checks so there was times when I had a lot of money on me, maybe eight hundred or a thousand dollars or so. Scot didn't like the thought of that so he went and got me a pistol. It was for protection if somebody tried to rob me. We both knew that I wasn't supposed to have a gun since I was a felon, but we figured takin the risk made sense. Wasn't like I was gonna get robbed, but havin a gun on me meant if I was, probably wouldn't get jacked when I flashed it and yelled that I was gonna shoot.

Scot even took me over to a gun range and taught me how to load it and shoot it and reload it again. We used to shoot at these little paper targets of the top of a man so I could practice shootin at his shoulders and head. You better not shoot nobody in the leg he used to tell me. If they are threatenin you or takin somethin of yours, shoot them dead in the face. We'll claim self-defense or somethin and say that it was either your life or theirs. So that's what we did. Anybody'll tell you that girls are better shots than boys, and let me tell you that I was a pretty damn good shot. Might not have always hit my target in the face, but wasn't often that my shots hit outside the target outline. I think even Scot was impressed. He been shootin down on his daddy's farm since he was a boy and every time I hit the target between the eyes or in the chest and not in the white of the paper, he would just smile and shake his head. It made me feel good to know he was proud of me.

Life was good for us for years. Scot was doin so good at Wal-Mart and my business was blowin up like I never thought. The girls was perfect and spittin images of they daddy, just a little darker and a whole lot prettier! Ha! I had got a little sick and couldn't work the way I used to for weeks. The girls was five and three, and in daycare, so I either stayed home most days or did light work along side my cleanin girls. Some of the money me and Scot saved meant that I could stay out of work longer than I probably would have, and that probably helped me get better faster.

I started back about four months after falling ill – doctor said it was tied to my allergies and bein around chemicals all day. It's only natural that I wish I could have spent more time with the girls lookin back on the time I did have with them, but in those times when it was just me, I learned more about myself and bein a momma and a wife than I ever thought. The brightness in my babies eyes and the way they needed me still makes me cry sometimes if I think about how we used to spend time after what we used to call school. Penelope and Rebecca was in daycare up at Bright Horizons and they was growin up right before our eyes and bein just the best sisters in the world. They was little mirror images of me and Shaniqua. Penelope could have started school when she turned four, but me and Scot thought it best to leave her out one more year so she could maybe catch up. Past that, I swear, Penelope was a much better big sister than I ever could have been that's for sure.

Life was coming close to perfect. But what I didn't know was that Scot had been reachin out and talkin to his mother. I ain't have the first clue about that. And from a man who told me that we didn't need to have a secret between us, he sure was keepin a monster from me. Because that's what I thought about his momma Carrie – I thought she was a monster. I never got over that letter she sent him. Never. And it wasn't my place to be the bigger person or say the right thing or apologize for nothin. If anybody, she should have come crawlin her ass to me to say how wrong she been and how wrong it was what she said about me and Scot.

Now, in the time just after Rebecca was born and I was recoverin from givin birth again, Scot got me in a weak moment and he asked me again and I finally agreed to marry him. Haha! I say weak moment because I was strung out on no sleep and Rocky Road. I thought the poor man must have also been losin his sight, because wasn't no way he still thought anythin positive about me. I was still big a long time after the pregnancy, and just about as big as ever when he asked me to marry him. I figured if he loved me as a whale, he'd love me if I ever got skinny again. I pictured myself draggin a wagon full of fat out of nowhere like Oprah did when she lost all that weight and looked like a million bucks in those skinny bitch jeans and that black sweater. We got married in a little ceremony in a pretty little chapel in Charlotte. Barbara was my bridesmaid and Bryon was Scot's best man. We only had about twenty people at our wedding and none of them was blood on either side. The girls cried the whole time, and me and Scot just smiled and laughed through the whole ceremony and it was wonderful.

Well, like I said he was keepin his secret talks with his momma to himself. He knew what I thought about her and he knew I was right to think what I did. I can't say whether or not he was right to keep the secret from me that he was talkin again to his momma. And I can't say that what I did was right, either. But what I do know is that if I ever got the chance to relive that night, I wouldn't change a damn thing.

☠♏☒♦

I found out that Scot had got his momma back in his life, and I exploded on him. I hadn't never cursed him before that day, and you could tell he was truly hurt. He was between a rock and a real goddam hard place, lovin his momma and his wife and his babies, wantin everybody to be right with one another. But like I told him, wasn't nothin good gonna come from him keepin me in the dark like that. It's a strange feelin, wantin to punch your man in the mouth and hug him at the same time. I swear it is. Lookin back on it, I guess that also meant he was talkin to his daddy. Hindsight, right?

I had always thought they lived maybe a ways away from Charlotte until he told me they had a place outside of Chester in South Carolina. That ain't a stones throw from Charlotte by way of 77 south. Didn't know why, but Scot actually drove us down there one Sunday afternoon after his wounds had healed – haha – and I'd gotten my feet under me again. He wanted me and Penelope and Rebecca to at least see where he was from, and to his mind maybe think that some day soon we'd all be down there celebratin a holiday or havin a summer party or somethin that he used to do with his parents and probably missed. Mind you, we'd been together for almost six years at this point. That's a long time to go without your momma.

All the way there, I was takin in everything. From the way my stomach felt thinkin what I'd do if maybe they was on the road and saw us and wanted us to stop, I knew I was nervous and had to get a hold of myself.

I remember the exit number and the simple couple turns it took to get to the driveway. They lived off the road, down a gravel driveway that we didn't dare go down. Scot made like he was gonna turn in and I slapped him across the chest. It was a lot harder than I intended and I apologized tellin him I was nervous and it just wouldn't be right for us to show up uninvited and without first clearin the air. He didn't say nothin all the way home.

It was at trial that I'd found out Scot had been home several times and seen his parents a little bit before Penelope was born, and kept goin in the years afterward – not so much after that nasty letter, but evidently pickin back up when the holidays was over. Maybe that's why he was always in a good mood. He had his whole family back together even though part of it didn't know and ain't never met the other. This little Sunday drive was a plan hatched by him and his momma, but never came to be because I was too shaken to go down the drive to the house. I sit and think about what could have been.

As it stands, life went back to normal for me and him and Penelope and Rebecca and the crazy life we had together. I actually wasn't back to work too long for good, and remember that I had left Mrs. Caroline's house about six o'clock and was racin to get to the daycare to pick up Penelope and Rebecca. They was real understandin at Bright Horizons and since the children had to be picked up by not too long after six and they knew sometimes I came from a long way to get them, they ain't never charged me for bein late. When I got to the daycare, I rushed inside and the receptionist greeted me at the door askin me why I'd come back. I said I ain't been there that day – Scot dropped them off that mornin. She said okay but that the girls wasn't there. They was checked out earlier that day. The receptionist said that she saw them leave with their grandmother, that Scot had left a note that mornin when he dropped them off that they'd get picked up by his mother. I felt myself first go weak and then I got hornets nest pissed.

Scot had told me that he was goin to pick up the girls and take them to dinner because I was goin to be workin later than normal that night. Mrs. Caroline was to have a dinner party the next day and she wanted everything just perfect. I thought it was gonna take longer to get everything spic and span, but I had another girl help me and we'd finished just about normal time. Since I ain't have a cell phone, I thought I'd catch Scot and the girls at the daycare when he was pickin them up and that we could have a family dinner. It would be nice to have a night off from cookin and I knew it would be a great surprise for Scot. Mrs. Caroline had paid me a tip in cash - $100 - and we could use some of that for dinner. He ain't count on me gettin off early, and he ain't count on me goin by the daycare.

I asked to see the sign out ledger and right there in blue pen was her name but it was scratched out over top and somebody wrote Scot's name but it wasn't his writin. The receptionist got this scared look on her face as I proceeded to cuss a blue streak around both Scot and Carrie. A woman I ain't know had come in on his permission and taken my kids somewhere I ain't never been and ain't ever plan on visitin. I said out loud for anybody to hear that that bitch was gonna die. Wasn't somethin I meant and wasn't somethin I ever expected to be used against me. I tore out of there and ran to my car. I was gettin my ass on 77 lickety split and I knew right where I was goin. That bitch is crazy if she thinks I'm lettin this happen. And I'ma deal with Scot when I see him, too. That's what I was thinkin.

It's the God's honest truth that I don't remember nothin about that drive into Chester. I was blind with rage and it's a wonder I ain't get pulled over even once for the way I was ridin that rocket to where I only guessed my kids would be. I might have gone home and waited if I thought anybody but Carrie had checked them out. Only me, Scot, Barbara and Bryon – the babies godparents – had the right to get them out of daycare. If Scot thought he was gonna pull a fast one on me, he had another thing comin. Momma Gloria always said you don't bullshit a bullshitter. You don't try and pull no tricks on somebody like me cause it's gonna end up bitin you in the ass. And he should have known not to pit a momma against another momma. Momma beats grandmomma every time and his wasn't fittin to be no exception to that rule.

I damn near turned on two wheels onto that gravel drive. Remember it takes an hour or so to get there, and I probably made it in forty or forty-five minutes. It had got dark by the time I'd got to Chester and I flipped on the high beams as I drove down toward the house. The drive was flanked with rows and rows of somethin. Might have been corn, might have been somethin else, I don't know. Probably wouldn't have been pretty in the daylight and probably would have been pretty if I hadn't been seein red.

The drive turned to asphalt and then it opened rather sudden to a cleared out area with a house to the left and a barn off in the distance to the right. When I left out of the daycare in a huff like I did, the receptionist called the Wal-Mart where Scot worked and told him that I didn't seem quite right, that I might have been mad. She testified that she heard the phone drop to the ground, he said oh goddammit what have I done, and it sounded like he was tearin out of there like I left the daycare. He couldn't have been no more than five or ten minutes behind me and he was haulin ass just like I was because he knew what I was capable of. In court, he said he'd been delayed about thirty minutes from goin to get the girls from his parents and would have had plenty of time to get them from them and take them to get dinner. I'd have never known a thing about it if I hadn't gotten my work done so quick and if I'd gone straight home afterward.

I jammed on those brakes and skidded my car to a halt. I got out lookin like I was some bad bitch from the movies with tire smoke comin up around me. The drive was a circle and I stopped right in front of the front door. Right as I started around the car the front door flew open and it was his daddy yellin at Scot to slow the hell down. When he realized it wasn't his son, but his babies momma racin toward him, he slammed the door real fast and locked it. They had these little windows on the side of the door that let you see who was standin on your porch before you opened the door and I smashed a couple of them. I kicked them in and went to unlock the door. Mind you, I ain't really have no idea where my kids was, but I figured they was in there. I hear Victor yellin to put the kids in the car. I got the front door open and just as I got inside, I felt a bat hit me in the stomach. I fell to the ground in some kind of awful pain. I look up and see Victor standin over me. I got about sixty pounds on him, and he looks like he about seventy years old. I got up on my hands and feet and launched myself into him, tacklin his ass, pinnin him to the floor. He'd fell next to a table with a little lamp on it and dragged it by the cord until it fell on my head. I punched him in the face like I had done Herbert all those years ago and he slapped me across the mouth and again across the face. He grabbed a piece of that shattered lamp and jabbed it into my side. I rolled off of him and grabbed at my waist. My hand pulled back bloody and told him that didn't do nothin but piss me off more.

Victor got up quick as he could and started to the back of the house. Maybe he was goin for the kitchen or maybe he was goin for a gun or knife, or maybe that's where my kids and Carrie were waitin in their car. I jumped up and ran back out the front door. I heard my Penelope askin where they were goin and where her momma was and I got fired up all over again. I ran to my trunk and popped it open to get to my gun. I ran to the right side of the house, where you could see the barn in the distance just as Carrie and Victor and my kids came backin out of the garage real quick. Victor acted like he was gonna run me over and slammed on the brakes when he seen the gun in my hand and I fired off a shot over them. He held his hands up in the air and I told him to get out of the car. Carrie's lookin at him, huddled in the back seat with my girls, clutchin the baby in her arms.

Victor puts the car in park over Carrie yellin at him to just run me over. You tricky bitch I yelled. I got 18 more bullets for your ass. Trust and believe I'ma use them if I have to. Give me back my goddam children! Victor starts gettin out of the car, his hands are still in the air like that's gonna make me put down my gun. What? What?! You took my goddam children, stole them without so much as sayin hello to me, you hit me in the stomach, slapped my face and dropped a lamp on me, stab my black ass and you want me give you mercy. Ain't no fuckin way. I can see Penelope cryin in the back seat and Carrie tryin to get her stop, coverin her mouth and she fightin back, tryin to get away. Victor starts walkin toward me askin if we can just talk this out. No hard feelins and nobody has to call the police and I won't go back to prison for breakin in their house and assaultin him.

I asked Victor if he was fuckin high because this wasn't somethin he had any control over. He was gonna give me my goddamed kids back, we was gonna leave and they'd never see us again. He kept walkin toward me and I told him to fuckin stop or I'd shoot him where he stood. Carrie is yellin for him to get back in the car, the girls is screamin their heads off cause they scared, Carrie is yellin that I ain't gonna shoot nobody, not especially with the girls watchin. A mother wouldn't do that to her kids she said. Victor turned around like he was gonna get back in the car and I told him again to give me my kids. He got to the car and put his hand on the door and I pulled the trigger again. I shot just over his head to tell him that I wasn't fuckin jokin. My damn kids right then or somebody was gonna die. And since I had the gun, wasn't gonna be me.

He turned back to me and was actually mad. Must have heard that bullet whiz above him. Guess Scot left out the part about me bein a crack shot. Had this look on his face like I was the one started all this. Motherfucker thought wasn't no way I'd do that and now he was pissed. He start walkin toward me with this look on his face and Carrie is screamin more and harder for him to get in the car. I told him to stop that I just wanted my girls and this would be over. I'm backin up kinda fast because I'm scared out of my mind. I don't want to shoot nobody. I just wanted to have my damn kids back in my car and break out. I hear him call me a dirty stupid bitch and that wasn't no way I was gettin these kids back because I wasn't fit to be no parent. He bent down and picked up somethin from the ground. It must have been some damn dirt or gravel or somethin I don't know. He tossed it at me to maybe distract me or somethin and started runnin at me.

I pulled the trigger and shot over his head again. And he kept runnin. So I steadied myself and in the second or so before he got to me, I put a bullet through his left cheek. Freaked me out cause he lunged at me and kinda fell on me, tryin to hold his body up and his head was blowed out the back. And then he just dropped to the ground. His head was mangled and he was bleeding and a lot of his brain was on the ground behind him and down his clothes. I knew he was dead. Ain't no way he survived that. I blinked for a hot second and heard Carrie screamin bloody murder. At the same time, I heard tires screechin and turned and saw a car haulin ass down that drive, gravel dust shootin into the air. Had to be Scot coming to the rescue. Red and blue lights and sirens was comin right behind him.

I turned back and saw Carrie still in the backseat handin my baby to my five year old and bucklin her belt. She was about thirty feet from me and started scramblin to get into the front seat. I started runnin toward her as she plopped into the drivers seat and put her car in gear. Scot came screamin up the drive and slammed on his brakes like I had. He jumped out of his car and stood ghost still and white at the sight of his dead daddy on the pavement. He starts screamin for me to put the gun down and that he was sorry he ain't told me about the plan. Please just put the gun down. He ran to his daddy to see if there was a pulse, if there was anything he could do to keep him alive.

Carrie lifted off the brakes about the time I made it to her and I yelled at her to stop the car. I shot into the drivers side window, across her face, and the bullet shattered the closed passenger window. She stomped her foot down on the gas and I pulled the trigger two more times. The car jumped forward real quick and then rolled slowly to a stop when it crossed the grass and got stuck in a little vegetable garden. I was runnin to the car to get my babies out and hold them. Carrie was strugglin to breath when I got to the car. Sounded like she was blowin milk bubbles but it was the air and blood comin out of her neck all at the same time. Somehow, she'd opened the door and fell on her hands and knees in the dirt. She leaned against the car and stared at me, bubblin and gaspin for more air.

My first public defender told me that if it hadn't been for that last shot, point blank to her heart, I probably could have just gotten life without parole. The third shot was sold to the jury like I executed her. I ain't one to split hairs, so…

I'd dropped the gun so I could grab my babies and hug them one last time. I knew I was gonna go away for a long time for what I did. Wasn't no escapin that. I unbuckled them and ran back toward my car. Scot ran right fuckin by me and his girls to check on his momma. He screamed like a little bitch when he got up to the car. Didn't even look at me or his babies, just ran right to his momma.

I didn't get far. Police and medics and whatever else had jammed the drive and grass and the police had their guns out and pointed at me to put my girls down and get on the ground. I ain't think they would shoot me with my babies in my arms, and for a hot goddam second I thought about rushin those motherfuckers and takin them with me to wherever it was beyond this life that I was destined to go. And I felt Penelope grippin me scared out of her mind and Rebecca was crying like she ain't never cried before and I realized they didn't have nothin to do with why we was in the position we was in right then and there. I turned to see Scot, who'd been tackled by the police and moved away from his dead momma. I looked back at the police and took a deep breath.

I kissed my girls on the cheeks and forehead and lips and rubbed their little faces and felt their soft skin with my nose and we cried together for a second. I put them on the ground and that's when I felt the shot go through my shoulder. I got thrown backward and remember how dark the sky was and how the stars changed from red to white to blue and back to red as the light bounced off the police cars and the ambulance and made the stars dance. I got rushed, I got handcuffed, and then I blacked out from the pain.

That was the last time I ever saw my girls in person.

The next time I saw Scot was the day he testified against me.

I never saw him again.

June 29 (5)

Dear Diary –

I don't know how I'm going to do this. That's what I was thinking as I sat in the visitation room waiting for them to bring Janine to me. My mouth was dry and I was having a difficult time concentrating on the speech I'd prepared the night before. The explanation to Janine and the explanation to myself for dropping out of her life so many years ago wasn't going to be something pleasant. I don't know why I thought that. I don't know why it would matter so much to Janine. And maybe it didn't. She'd never asked me about the time I wasn't with her, when I wasn't able to comfort or guide her. Or maybe have kept her off of the path she'd traveled and ultimately committed a crime so egregious, there was no other punishment but death.

Those were the things I was thinking to myself until the door opened. And then my mind went blank. I was numb.

This woman, this shining example of resilience and fortitude, facing the last five days of her life, bounded into the visitation room and was actually smiling. Instinctively, I smiled, too. And then I burst into tears before Janine could even sit. I hadn't uttered a word of my soliloquy, and she is already comforting me. God truly works in mysterious ways.

I gathered myself and looked at her. The smile was gone, having been replaced by an inquisitive look, and for Janine that also meant a skeptical scowl. "What the hell wrong with you?" was what she asked me. I smiled and told her that I'd always love her. "That don't answer my question." Classic Janine.

I told her that I had something I needed to tell her. There was something eating at me for decades that I needed to confess. Without hesitating, Janine's face turned serious and she said, "How long has it been since your last confession, Sister?" And she smiled. She wasn't making this any easier. "Go on then. I only got 15 minutes today cause these bitch ass guards don't want me no place but my cell. Talk fast. By the look on your face, might take longer than that if you don't start now."

My speech was long-forgotten so I just started talking from my heart.

"I haven't been a nun recognized by the Church in over three decades, Janine. You shouldn't be calling me Sister because I don't deserve the title." She said nothing. So I continued. "I have kept things hidden from you, things about me and my life, that have been too painful and embarrassing to tell you. I am ashamed of that behavior, especially in light of the counseling I've provided you over the years." Still nothing. Janine is looking at me as though I'm an actor on television and she is waiting for the seminal moment before reacting. It frustrated me, but I didn't feel at that moment I had any right to assign emotions to her feelings. I took a deep breath and said, "I have been a heroin addict since I was 15, the same year I was raped at some point after I'd overdosed." Janine closed her eyes, put her hands to her face and began to weep. It was so much more than unexpected, I was actually caught off-guard for a moment.

"Momma Gloria was raped, too," was all she said, still weeping, connecting the singular experience shared by what I'd gathered were the two women in her life that were the most impactful on her in one way or another.

I reached out to touch her, and just as I did the guard yelled at me violently to not touch the prisoner! I jolted but Janine was rock solid, inquisition creeping over her face, as she wiped her eyes. I put my hands back on the table.

"Yes, she was," I said. "And it is a horrible feeling to recall, a terrible process through which you have to try and work to be sane. Some women make it and some women are crushed by its effects, its aftermath, its solemnity. But something wonderful came out of such a tragic experience for your mother and that was you."

"I'd rather have never been born if I could have kept her from that. Ain't nobody should have to go through that."

No, I replied. No one should. "I was kind of lucky, even though that is a horrible choice of words. I say that because through my haze and torrent of emotions whirling around me, I was able to pick out one of the ones who raped me." Janine looked at me and rubbed her eyes and nose.

"You caught him?" she asked. "Who was he? How old were you again? What happened?"

For what I hoped would be the final retelling of this sinister tale, I filled Janine in on every detail I could. How I'd skipped out of school, how I'd gotten stoned on Brad, how I'd passed out in the old church building. The faces of the boys were unrecognizable; their voices were foreign to me. But there was something familiar and comforting about the voice of the last one. I had no idea how long I'd been there, laying on the floor after the last boy had had his way with me. I didn't know what time it was or where this man's voice was coming from. But I knew the tone and texture of his words. Again, I felt my dress moved up and my legs spread and someone enter me without my permission. I was being taken again and still Brad wouldn't let me stop him. It wasn't until years later, after I'd gotten locked down in rehab for the second or third time, that my counselor helped me put the images and words together. I could see his face, Janine. And I knew was that he was going to die for what he'd done.

"Did he?" was all she asked.

I looked at the guard who was looking right back at me. I moved on. I told her that in the time she was in Leath for the theft charge, I was in and out of facilities, finally landing in the hands of God, directing my life toward His work. The heroin no longer controlled me. And I was no longer angry at my attacker. Romans 12:19 tells us that "Beloved, never avenge yourselves, but leave it to the wrath of God, for it is written, 'Vengeance is mine, I will repay, says the Lord.'" So I did nothing.

After I'd become a nun, I was placed in my home parish and assigned to work under an established priest, Father Tervis, family friend, family priest, and an unforgettable mentor. Oh, Janine, I learned so much about loving the Lord and about how to serve parishioners from him. I rose quickly within the ranks of the Church and at one point was even granted an audience with the Bishop in recognition of the charity work we'd organized through the parish. I was with him for four years, from 21 to just after I turned 25. This was about the time you were in Leath and I wasn't there for you.

There was always something so comforting about him and I longed to be closer to him, tempting my lessons against the temptations of the body, ignoring the fact that he was not only my Monsignor, but some thirty-five years my senior. Lust is powerful, and there is no more lustful position you'll find than that which I faced with Father Tervis.

I was thinking too much about things I shouldn't have been where Father Tervis was concerned, all the while doing whatever I could to be close to him, to learn from him and longed to be in his presence. I don't know if he knew that, but somehow he picked up on my advances and without explanation one evening in his office, we succumbed to my passion and his superiority.

It was not what I expected it to be, Janine, I said. It was violent – more so than I'd imagined for months as I gazed at him, torturing my soul. It was as if he were both teaching me a lesson for having found myself at the gates of hell, the devil guiding my hands and body, but also in some way as though he were experiencing a release of his own. It was frightening and not passionate.

"Like you was gettin raped all over again," Janine said, eyebrow raised. And I agreed.

I told Janine that the most humiliating part was what he kept repeating during the three or four minutes he was having sex with me. I committed it to memory and looked it up after he finished and made me excuse myself from his office, only after reminding me of the power he commanded as Monsignor. It was Matthew 5:28. "But I say to you that everyone who looks at a woman with lustful intent has already committed adultery with her in his heart."

Janine just shook her head and said, "That's the same shit you heard before, ain't it?"

I explained to Janine that it wasn't long after that, probably a couple of weeks that I'd found Brad again. And a couple weeks after that, I picked up one night and quietly left the parish and the Church completely. I moved around a little bit in this van I'd bought, kicked Brad out of my life one more time, and I'dgotten my certificate as a counselor. I decided I was going to help women like myself to deal with being raped and maybe with drug addiction if I could stay clean. I hopped from treatment center to treatment center over the next however many years. I was actually sitting at a rest stop somewhere right outside Greensboro after an interview for some job I didn't get when I saw in the paper that a woman had been arrested for murdering her in-laws. I told her that my mouth fell agape when I read that it was her. After being apart for so long, God had brought us back together again. I talked my way into becoming a counselor at the Correctional Facility, I sat day after day in the courtroom during your trial, like I had done so many years before, and when you were convicted and sentenced, I applied to be your counselor. We'd saved each other once, maybe we could do it again.

"But wait," she said. "You said nothin to nobody about that creep who raped you, the old guy Tervis?" I shook my head. "And you quit bein a nun over that shit?" I nodded my head. Janine squinted and looked at me, head tilted. "So why you got that look on your face when I walked in? You got me cryin over Momma Gloria bein raped. What gives? What's this secret you tryin to tell me about?"

I didn't know what to say. I had just told her that I wasn't a nun, despite my not insisting my patients call me otherwise, and I admitted to being a heroin junkie and sleeping with my boss and mentor. I was flabbergasted.

“You lookin to get some kind of sympathy, Sister? Or fake Sister, whoever you are?” She smiled. “Girl you just like me: human. You think cause you used to get dolled up in all that black shit and you quote scripture like it’s stank breath comin out of your mouth that you were better than everybody else and that makes your fall from fuckin grace worse than anybody else? Bitch, please. I ain’t got pity for you. But I also ain’t got nothin but love for you.” That through me for a loop. “You human, Sister. We fuck up. We pay for it. And we go on about our goddam business. I’ma always love you for what you got me through when I was comin up. I’ma always love you for what you tried to do in getting me off death row. I’ma always love you for stayin with me and talkin to me and listenin to my stories about the girls and life and Scot and whatever else. Always gonna love you for that shit. You weren’t there for me when the heavy shit was goin down, no. But I wasn’t there for you, neither. That’s life. I killed a man and his wife, in they front yard, cause they wasn’t smart enough to give me my damn kids back. I’ma die for that shit in five days. But you gotta let this martyr shit go, honey. It ain’t a good look.”

And that’s why I love her. I pour out my heart, details of my life I’d kept hidden for decades. And all she tells me is that we’re human and she loves me no matter what. The guard cleared his throat and motioned for Janine to start back to her cell. She stood and with a straight face said, “I’ma pray for you, Sister.” My heart sang with pride, I beamed uncontrollably, and my eyes welled up. And then she said, “Haha, I ain’t fuckin doin that, Sister. That was a joke. But I’ma love you until the day I die. You been more momma to me in or out of my life than Momma Gloria ever was. And that means more to me than you ever gonna know.”

I couldn’t stop crying.

1 Corinthians 13:7 “Love bears all things, believes all things, hopes all things, endures all things.”

June 30 (4)

Let me tell y'all somethin. And I'm talkin to you Sister. At whatever point after I'm dead and y'all go back and read this book, if Chocolate can get the shit published, know that Sister is all things to me. Momma, sister, girlfriend, everything. After I got locked up, I ain't have my kids, Barbara stopped visitin real quick when she said Scot and Bryon and her other friends started givin her down the road about me, and I was alone with nobody but Sister. And that's how it's been for a long time.

I saw her again today, and we can't believe time is windin down so quick. It wasn't that damn long ago we was sittin in the visitation room and I got my letter and she told me to write. Goddam that seems like it was just yesterday. Ask yourself what you would do if you only had thirty days to live.

I told Sister one of the things I missed most about bein a momma and wife was cookin for them, makin sure they was fed and had a full belly. That kinda turned to what I wanted for my last meal. That was somethin I never thought about. What's the last thing I'd want to eat before dyin. I told Sister that I didn't want nothin. I couldn't think of nothin and I wasn't gonna use whatever time I had left comin up with it. She asked me to think about it another way. What would you make for your girls and Scot, people you love, if it was the last thing they'd ever gonna eat. I guess I perked up at the thought, puttin myself back in my old kitchen. I closed my eyes and could smell what I was makin for my girls and my man.

Some good fried chicken, honey. That sweet potato casserole Scot like so much. Some juicy ass Collards with hot sauce. Oooh, my mouth waterin again just sayin the words. Momma Latta cole slaw recipe I got off of Momma Gloria without her lookin one day. And some of them light and fluffy rolls ain't nobody know how to make but Momma Gloria long, long time ago. I explained everything to Sister like I was in the kitchen doin it myself. And I was surprised how easy it came back to me since it'd been so long since I could do it.

That's what I'd make my babies and my Scot, I told her. That, to me, is love. Love ain't always somethin you feel or you hear. Love has a taste, too. Love is sweet and crispy and tangy, child. Love makes you feel warm and makes you excited. Love makes you smack your lips. Shit, sometime love even makes you wanna smack your momma! Haha! Love feeds the soul and keeps you alive. If you put all that on a plate, you know you doin somethin right.

So I don't want no last meal. I think maybe the thought of cookin again for my babies and my Scot is all I'ma need to get me through.

Yep, that's all I need.

Sister was writin like a fiend as I was talkin. I guess she gonna put that in the book or somethin. Been a long time since she wrote down what I said after I told her not to so long ago. Whatever.

There goes my mouth waterin again!

July 1 (3)

Sister didn't show up for the session today. I got 30 minutes a day to talk to somebody other than myself and she don't show up. Three days left and that's all I am to her.

That motherfucker of a guard told me today I was gettin measured for my casket and that he hoped they had a strong horse to pull me to the grave.

I looked at him and told him that me and Maya Angelou didn't think he was shit. "Phenomenally. Phenomenal woman, that's me."

July 2 (2)

Chocolate showed up out of the blue today. The door to the visitation room opened and I was expectin to see Sister. She missed the time yesterday and I was goin to give her a little ribbin at first and then make up real quick. But it wasn't her, it was Chocolate.

My first thought was that maybe he'd been able to get the execution stopped, maybe that the letter writin deal actually worked. The look on his face told me otherwise. I swear I wish people'd stop walkin in here with the look. He had a piece of paper or somethin in his hand and sat down. He slid it across the table at me and I just looked at him and asked what it was. Chocolate told me it was a letter and I told him I could see that and for him to tell me what it said. He wouldn't. And that made me real nervous.

I don't know what's gonna come of the letter after I'm dead so I'ma write here what it says.

"My dearest Janine. How I love you. For the longest time, you were the only one I had left in the world. Our parents are dead and gone. You were my sister in every way imaginable, except through the sharing of blood. The Lord gave you to me in an hour where I was losing my way; the clarity of shepherding lost and damaged souls toward His favor shall hold me and keep me through my journey to and throughout everlasting life in the kingdom of my Lord and Savior.

"Some would ask me why I chose to spend my life inside the walls of a prison, ministering to and counseling women many of whom society had cast aside, rightfully or not, for their crimes. There isn't another way to explain that, to enunciate the truth behind my conviction and purpose, my commitment to these women and myself…there is no other way to explain it other than to say that I felt as though I deserved to be there, as well, bound by personal conviction and self-imposed sentence. I was as much a prisoner to reality as were the precious and wayward women who looked to me for a lighted path. Helping others understand the beauty they possess and helping them blossom from whatever depths they originated was something significant to me. It was significant that I was the one on which they leaned, as I leaned on God for my own assistance. I leaned on Him when I didn't think He loved me, when I didn't feel worthy of the love of another, when I thought life's meaning and my ability to serve the Lord had diminished. The secrets of addiction and of my true self having voluntarily divested myself from the Church, from my first love, humped me over at the shoulder burdening me mercilessly.

"There were two things I did not tell you yesterday, one of which I must reserve judgment for only God. For in John 1:9 it reads that if we confess our sins, He is faithful and just and will forgive us our sins and purify us from all unrighteousness.

"Brad found me again after all this time, and I dare say I'm glad he has. My penance has come to an end and I shall be free this night. The Lord signaled to me that my time helping you on earth had come to an end. In homage, I prepared tonight to the best of my ability that which you said you would feed your loved ones on their last day. Forgive my having probed you for details that day, but I thought it only fitting that my Last Supper would be one of your own.

I will go now and wait for you, Janine. I will await your Heavenly arrival and shower you for eternity with the love of a sister, a mother, and friend. Do not weep for me because we will see each other soon. The Lord is OUR shepherd. And, yes, WE will dwell in the house of the Lord forever.

"Therefore, if anyone is in Christ, he is a new creation; the old has gone, the new has come!" (2 Corinthians 5:17)

In Christ's name,
Sister

Chocolate looked at me cryin and must have wondered if he ought to tell me this last part or not. I was already damned crushed. Spit it out, honey, I told him. Just fuckin say what you got on your mind.

He sat up a bit and swallowed real hard. Chocolate told me Sister had left a suicide note for the police, too. It told them there was a body hidden in a shallow grave under the crawl space of her house. I damn near passed out when he said that. He kept on. The Wake County coroner ruled last night that the body is the missin rat bastard Catholic priest, Monsignor Jeremy Tervis, solvin the case of his disappearance and suspected murder more than thirty years ago. Ain't that some shit?

She got him back. Been carryin his body around like a cross for decades. Lord only knows why and how. But she got him.

I'm kind of happy for her. But all I can really think about is that my girl is gone. And I'm all alone again right when I need her the most.

I just don't have words right now. My heart is broken into a thousand little pieces. I just don't have no words at all.

July 3 (1)

I don't want to write nothin today. I know that sound selfish as all hell, but it's true. Only problem is if I don't say nothin today, and I can't say nothin after tomorrow, what's left? I mean I got a lot more to say. Whatever else I got on my mind between now and then just gonna stay unwritten. I'ma take the last of me and my thoughts and dreams and shit that scares me and makes me laugh to the grave. Whatever I don't write today gonna be it. Game over.

Not sure how I'ma sleep tonight. The radio's playin Piano Sonata No. 14 in C Sharp Minor. If you don't know it by that name, you know it for "Moonlight Sonata." It's one of my favorites. I think maybe it's the last song I want to hear. I think that'll be a good memory to hold on to until tomorrow. Crazy shit, but…I wonder what'll happen to my radio when I'm dead. Guess that's really no matter now.

I think before I stop and put this pen down and leave whatever sense of my life and myself to the world to thank or lie on or whatever, I can't leave without talkin to my girls. I owe the last words I ever write to them. If this gets published, I want them to know they was on my mind every damn day of they lives – whether I was holding them or not.

Penelope, baby, you was the first and always gonna be special. I loved the way you felt and smelled and even cried as a baby. I watched you grow up into a beautiful and smart little girl. And a great big sister. Rebecca, you don't know this cause you was too young to remember, but you gave your big sister hell. Feisty and strong-willed, you reminded me of what it must have been like for Shaniqua when she was comin up behind me. Don't never take that sister bond for granted. Love each other and be there even when you don't want to be. I learned that lesson the hard way and paid for it all my life. If you don't know nothin else, know that momma loved you. More than you could ever know. I loved you so so much. And I'm sorry for everything you got put through for what I did. I don't have no right to ask, but please don't hate me. Maybe that's what Sister wanted me to teach – learn from me so you don't end up nothin like me. Make somethin of yourself, do somethin you can be proud of in life. Have babies and love on them and cook for them and teach them how to be women. Protect them from the world until you just can't any longer, and then try some more. Love a good man who loves you right back. Let him treat you like a queen but treat him just as much like a king and do your best not to keep nothin between you.

I think – I think I gotta go now. The last words I write will be yours and the last thoughts in my brain will be of you and the last words out of my mouth will be your names. I'ma love you now and forever. My Penelope. My Rebecca.

Editor's Notes
Susan D. McLachlan, Executive Editor
West Range Publishing

When Mary Ellen Fitzgerald (the woman you know as Sister) first came to me with this idea of turning the life story of Janine into an actual autobiography, I did not know how things would develop, escalate, and so dramatically tear at the very fiber of my being. I must tell you that I knew Mary Ellen for more than twenty-five years. And in that time, I saw the best and worst sides of her, as she was both my friend and counselor in Christ. Her loss is devastating on innumerable levels. But her indelible mark on this world, and those who inhabit it for better or for worse, is what you have read; the glimpse into her life was but a taste, and the lasting impression she had on those she touched will be her eternal legacy. Part of that legacy is Amethyst Janine Montgomery-Branch.

Over the weeks it took to convince me and my senior editors of the power and, quite honestly, the marketability of this woman's journey, I more fully understood the attraction I had to Mary Ellen as a person, as well as a lost and compassionate soul. In those quiet, stolen moments we shared over coffee or a weekend dinner, she relaxed and exhibited a charismatic nature, gesturing and retelling wonderful stories. She was full of contentment about her role in life, and I was lucky enough to experience, quite honestly, a smattering of what made her special to those she touched. It was a juxtaposition to the inner turmoil she was so very adept at hiding.

The internal mandate to preach the gospel as well as she could, and as honestly as she did just that given everything that befell her, knowing what I know now after having read her own hand, only intensifies my own personal emotions. I tingle when thinking of those I've met or with whom I've spoken in passing, never to give them or their life's experience a second thought, and it saddens me. I sensed in Mary Ellen that she was a woman so fragile and damaged, herself, a soul who lived a life of piety and selflessness, one only a true and delivered child of God could sustain. Her two addictions were powerful, to say the least;

one of which ultimately killed her, and the other which comforted her as she made her way from this lifetime into the everlasting peace she longed for.

It is rare when you meet someone that you know when your journey with them, your walk with them, as it were, will end. I began this journey, Janine's final chapter, with Mary Ellen believing that we would be celebrating the life of someone who was bombastic, loving, tragic, intelligent and street smart, motherly, and so very broken in ways neither of us – so I thought at the time – could fully appreciate, given the chasm separating our divergent experiences. As I came to know Janine through communication with Mary Ellen, and as I absorbed page after page, I was more and more intrigued.

At first, I had been determined to meet this woman, this person who had been condemned to die at the hands of the state. I wanted to look into her eyes and, for myself, discern what it was that lead her down the path she had so-well traveled. To touch her rough aged hands, even if only in my imagination, to hear what her voice sounded like, to smell her scent and to move my body imperceptibly with the undulations of her speech, to know this woman, was what I thought I needed to make the story more meaningful and weighted. A real and physical connection to this person would be the key to my finally getting the buy-in I needed to…to what? Accomplish what in meeting her and pulling her away from her work, further scrutinizing her in fishbowl of condemnation? How selfish of me.

And that's when I decided that I should never meet her. I should never be so arrogant as to waste the little time she had left to satisfy my own grotesque curiosity, to quench whatever it was that made me turn her pages immediately after Mary Ellen or Janine's attorney had sent them to me and I squirreled away in my office, printed copies in hand, falling more deeply into her story, and more deeply in love with someone I would never know. The urge to correct her grammar and spelling and outrageously vulgar language and sentence structure faded away as I read more, understanding that this was a guide, in her own authentic words, through a life Mary Ellen so aptly said that only Janine could describe. What you've read is exactly how it was written and sent to me.

It was my decision, however, to combine Mary Ellen's words with Janine's. I hadn't been aware of Mary Ellen's intention of writing out her own last days, and was taken aback when they arrived in my office, bound in a simple pile and dated to follow Janine's timeline. It would have been criminal not to include her writing, pairing their equally cathartic prose. The expressions of each are powerful and leave an impression so lasting, so thirsty for recognition and celebrity as would have been criminal to allow them, each just as important as the other, to fade away into obscurity on their own. Mary Ellen and Janine were important to each other as people, their lives each dependent upon the other at times, and so, too, now would their words.

It was also my decision to attend her execution, and it was my decision to include the last moments of Janine's life on earth and the unimaginable and perilous journey she walked. It is a decision which will haunt me for the remainder of my days.

July 4 (0)

I had never been to an execution. That might be a strange thing for someone to say, and it smacks of something chilling and silly and ignorant, as though it is possible for someone, for anyone, to say anything to the contrary. I did not know what to do with myself or my restless emotions. I was at one point suddenly hyperaware of my own existence as I, along with the fifteen or twenty other witnesses, prepared for something which heretofore would have seemingly been imaginable. I would have just as soon told you with full constitution that I had planned to swim on the face of the sun before I found myself in a North Carolina federal prison counting down the last minutes of someone's life.

We'd gathered an hour before in a stale waiting room to sign some documents and attest to the business we had in witnessing what was going to happen. We sat there until precisely twenty minutes before midnight, each politely smiling at one another, no one introducing themselves or making small talk. The guard stood very erect but bored in the corner by the door, clearly having drawn the short straw in babysitting us. Legs were shaking and you could feel the uncertainty some felt in attending. None of the witnesses were African American, so I assumed none of those in attendance were family. No one asked why I was there, and I returned the favor. I snapped to attention when the guard said it was time to go. We were to make our way now to the viewing room.

The small room was curved, somewhat like an auditorium in miniature, making use of every bit of available space. Each of us walked very deliberately inside, our lives never to be the same once we exited, that we knew for sure. Two rows of plush chairs in a sedate blue fabric, the second row slightly elevated behind the first, were sandwiched between the wall behind them and an imposing black curtain in front of them. We sat down, still not speaking to one another. I wondered what compulsion had brought me to my seat. And I remembered how I'd become absorbed in Janine's world. It was a connection I knew in my heart to be singular; out of everyone in the room I alone had a true and personal window into her very being. I did not know, and never could know everything about this woman brought into my world rather innocuously, but I knew more and cared more deeply for her than my fellow witnesses. Of that I was, and remain, sure.

The bright lights of the witness room were turned down, and a cool torrent of air began to snake its way across each of us. The crackle of a sound system coming online was off-putting and I realized that not only would I see her last moments, but that they would be accompanied by something of a macabre soundtrack. Our babysitter continued to watch over us, adjusting a volume knob on the wall until he found the level which he thought was comfortable for us.

Without any warning, the black curtain was whisked open – split down the middle, each portion gliding quickly to the periphery of our views, and causing several of us, men and women, alike, to gasp. It was here. It was happening. We could neither stop time altogether, nor turn back the clock such that an escape could be formulated or carried out.

Whether consciously or not, I immediately thought of Mary Ellen when the chamber was revealed to us. Spartan and bright white, there was a purity and calmness in its design, utilitarian to a fault. A single bed or table structure sat alone in the middle of the room, elevated on a thick, sturdy shaft which could rise or fall to make it easier for those administering the chemicals to reach the condemned. I thought of Mary Ellen because the position of the arms, splayed out to the sides of the bed, feet strapped closely together at the end of the bed, would position the prisoner similarly to Jesus on the Cross. Forgive them Father, I said out loud, for they know not what they do.

An EKG monitor, a smaller rudimentary metal table, and an office chair were the only other pieces of furniture present. An oddity to me, this being my first and hopefully only execution, was a row of telephones mounted on the wall. The last phone was marked with a sign labeled, "Governor's Office." It was ten minutes to midnight. I prayed that phone would ring.

A door on the far side of the chamber opened and that's when I first saw Janine. I couldn't help but begin to cry. The descriptions of herself were leaping off the page, punching me in the face with crispness and curiosity. The impact of her size hit me first and I was awed by how she dominated the room. A woman to my right handed me tissues and we held hands, sitting in a room full of people but clearly not wanting to be alone as we watched.

Janine was pretty to me. I saw a tender woman, on in years, and certainly not a monster, not someone capable of doing what she described in her memoirs. Wearing the state-provided plain brown dress she was handed earlier that day, she stopped suddenly when the door swung out of her way. Her expression dropped when saw the table upon which she would die. The woman next to me and I gripped each other's hands tighter. I could hear her sobbing slightly. I looked deeply at Janine and I imagined her listening to one of her piano concertos, or maybe what she remembered her children's laughter sounding like, anything she could to calm her nerves. And then to my complete surprise, she did something I still can't believe I saw: she smiled. She took a long, deep breath, and smiled. It wasn't toothy, and she wasn't happy, but it was a smile that told me a peace had come over her. Janine's time was at hand, and she had accepted it with grace.

I began to cry fully as she was strapped to the table, a guard at each of her extremities, and another ensuring the torso straps were secure. I'm not sure if anyone else noticed it, but the guard securing her left hand lingered a moment, an instant in time, and met Janine's eyes with his. You're going to be okay, his eyes said to her; I know, was her touching silent response.

An IV was placed in each arm and the warden stepped forward to ask if Janine had any last words.

What does one say when you know that it will be the last verbal communication ever to pierce your lips, ever to land in the ears of anyone listening? Is it something practiced? Is it something rude or vulgar and dismissive? Accusatory or damning or mean-spirited? Do you go to your grave with a lighter heart or an unburdened conscience?

Picking her head up enough to look into the one-way mirror that was the pane of glass separating her from the witness room she said, "My name is Amethyst Janine Montgomery-Branch. I love my children. And I would die a thousand times again and again to keep them safe." Janine began to tear and laid her head back down and said, "I'm comin to you, Sister. We got a lot more to talk about. I got a lot more to say. My Penelope. My Rebecca." She felt the rush of the saline solution flooding her body, and she closed her eyes.

Sodium thiopental was administered first and Janine, mercifully, fell into a very deep, restful sleep. For that I was grateful. Pavulon, an incredibly potent muscle relaxer came next, paralyzing her diaphragm and lungs. Potassium chloride was the last drug to be administered, blocking all electrical signals and inducing fatal cardiac arrest.

Flat line. One steady, high-pitched note squealed from the EKG monitor for a full minute. No one moved. We all just stared at her, lying still on the table. Waiting. And she was gone.

The attending physician gave time of death as July 4th, 12:08 am.

☠♏☒♦

Janine's funeral in a picturesque and peaceful cemetery off of Glenwood Road in Raleigh was attended by me, Gonzales, and the priest performing the ceremony. An ornate pink & gold casket with a matching marble marker were said to have been donated anonymously.

The bouquets of vibrant white and yellow carnations adorning the top of the casket all but swallowed the single card laid gently across them. It read simply:

"We love you. We forgive you." - Penelope, Rebecca, and Shaniqua.

The End